Take the problem of what to do with captured prisoners-of-war when they do not breathe the same atmosphere as you do, and the chances are you'll come up with the answer: put them on a planet where they can breathe; leave a satellite monitor to see that they don't try to escape, and leave them to their own resources.

This is the situation James White poses in his new novel, and we doubt that any reader will be surprised to find that the prisoners immediately start thinking of escape. Some of them, that is—others say there is no chance of getting away and they set about settling down for the rest of their lives. Almost inevitably, the two groups clash . . .

Open Prison is more than just an interplanetary novel of escape—as the situation develops we see the reasons and motives for men's actions—why they must ever strive for the impossible or why they simply give up. In a word, speculative adventure at its best.

TOM BOARDMAN JR.

Also by JAMES WHITE

HOSPITAL STATION
STAR SURGEON
THE WATCH BELOW
DEADLY LITTER
ALL JUDGEMENT FLED
THE ALIENS AMONG US

and published by CORGI BOOKS

James White

Open Prison

CORGI BOOKS
TRANSWORLD PUBLISHERS LTD
A National General Company

OPEN PRISON

A CORGI BOOK 552 08591 X

Originally published in Great Britain by
The New English Library Ltd.

PRINTING HISTORY

New English Library edition published 1965
Corgi edition published in 1970

This book is set in Pilgrim 10 pt.

Corgi Books are published by Transworld Publishers, Ltd.,
Cavendish House, 57–59 Uxbridge Road, Ealing,
London, W.5.

Made and printed in Great Britain by
Richard Clay (The Chaucer Press), Ltd., Bungay, Suffolk.

To
WALTER WILLIS
for all the reasons usually mentioned in a Dedication,
and more

CHAPTER ONE

When Warren had been extricated along with the other survivors of the erroneously named *Victorious* and made a prisoner of war he had thought that he knew what to expect, his expectations being based on the knowledge of how enemy POWs were handled by his own side.

With the other officers he had been moved to an enemy heavy cruiser and confined in one of its storage compartments, into which had been pumped what the enemy thought was an Earth-like atmosphere and where there was introduced at regular intervals substances which were the enemy's idea of what human beings ate. The air had had to be breathed but the food could only be eaten after the processes of starvation were well advanced. Then had come the expected series of transfers between supply ships returning from the battle area until eventually they found themselves being herded aboard a vessel of tremendous size which was in orbit around a planet. Within a few hours they were moved again, this time to a ship which was obviously a ferry, and now they were landing.

But on the final approach Warren was able to see that the planetary surface was green and heavily forested and that its night side showed no trace of artificial illumination—two facts which, considering the enemy's marked preference for dry worlds and harsh, blue-white lighting, came as a surprise to him. He was still wondering about it when the ship landed in a clearing and they were directed to the airlock and down a ladder which had not been made for human feet, on to grass still smouldering from the effects of the tail-blast. Nobody followed them out of the ship and neither did they appear to be under any form of restraint, which surprised Warren even more.

But all he could think about at that moment was the sheer joy of breathing air, that was clean and fresh and tainted only by the not unpleasant smell of burnt grass, so that these odd happenings did not worry him unduly. Then above him the ship emitted a low, humming sound. The ladder retracted suddenly and the outer seal of the lock began to swing closed.

'Run!' said somebody harshly.

Seconds later the ship took off with a sound like a continuous crack of doom and a blast of heat which, because their reactions were fast, was horribly uncomfortable instead of being instantly lethal. And even though the dwindling thunder from above told them they were safe, they didn't stop running until they reached the trees.

Long before they had their breaths back they were all trying to talk, and some of the language was not lady-like even though it was one of the ladies present who was using it. Warren looked slowly around the tragically small group which had survived the destruction of one of the mightiest battleships ever built. At the twenty-six officers in the green battledress uniforms devoid of all insignia or decorations, whose anonymity had been a ruse originally intended to confuse the enemy as to the relative importance of prisoners but which was now simply a matter of tradition. Just as it was traditional for the female half of a ship marriage to retain her own name so as to avoid the confusion of having two officers with the same name aboard ship. But there were no conventions to guide them in their present situation, Warren thought, as he listened to them vocalizing some of the thoughts which were going through his own mind at that moment. He did not say anything himself because there was nothing constructive he could say, and he could not have gotten a word in edgewise anyway.

'Why the stinking, lousy *Bugs* . . .!'

'This isn't a POW camp! They've marooned us here, without food or . . . or anything . . .!'

'They tried to kill us with their tail-flare . . .!'

'I'm not so sure about that,' a quieter voice said amid the uproar. 'The Bugs have never been deliberately cruel. There has to be a reason for all this . . .'

'The reason being,' another voice put in, 'that after sixty years of war they've grown to dislike us?'

'Very funny. But I still say . . .'

'Why they did it isn't very important at the moment,' a quiet, competent-sounding voice immediately identifiable as belonging to Major Fielding joined in. 'If we have been marooned, the first problem is to ensure our immediate survival . . .'

Ruth Fielding was a small, dark-haired girl who had been the medical officer and psychologist aboard *Victorious*. She was the type who could fly into a tizzy at some trifling upset and yet remain completely and utterly calm when everything and everybody around her was going to Hell on horseback. Warren had never been able to make up his mind whether this odd but very valuable aspect of her character was due to courage or sheer contrariness.

'. . . We must build shelters,' she continued quietly, 'and arrange protection against the weather and possibly dangerous animals. We must find water, search for edible plants and animals, fashion weapons . . .'

While she was speaking everyone began looking at the surrounding greenery, at the tight, almost spherical clumps of bushes whose shadows might conceal anything and at the tall, proud trees with their yellow-veined bark and leaves like big green seashells. From some of the branches brown, hairy fruit hung, or possibly they were parasitic growths or nocturnal creatures asleep for the day. The insects were too small to be seen, but as the thunder of the departing ship died away they could be heard droning to themselves.

And when they had finished looking around them the crew began glancing furtively at Warren, plainly wondering if his vast fund of tactical experience equipped him to handle this sort of problem. Because they were all intelligent and highly-trained people who would not be thrown into a panic by the immediate problems of survival which Fielding was mentioning. Many of them would already be considering the longer-range, Warren knew, already thinking in terms of the second and third generation while she was still making her final point.

'. . . Because our observations on the way down,' she concluded in a voice which seemed loud only because everybody else was holding their breath, 'make it pretty certain that we have this planet all to ourselves.'

Nobody spoke for a long time. No slightest breath of wind stirred the alien leaves and even the insects seemed to join momentarily in making the silence complete. Then the stillness was shattered by the sudden rattle of drums from the forest around them, the measured though erratic beat making it plain that intelligence of some kind was being transmitted. To the drum-beats was added the sound of whistles blowing and distant shouts, and an unmistakably human figure was running through the trees towards them.

'Oh, well,' said Fielding in a highly embarrassed voice, 'maybe we *don't* have the planet all to ourselves . . .'

The running figure slowed as it approached, from a sprint to something which was not so much a fast walk as a ceremonial quick march. After one glance around the group he marched unhesitatingly towards Warren and came to a halt before him. There he tore off one of the tightest, smartest salutes that Warren had ever seen.

'I am Lieutenant Kelso,' he said crisply. 'Are you the senior officer of this party, sir?'

Before replying, Warren looked the lieutenant slowly up and down. He noted the details of the kilt which the other wore, the calf-length boots and the sundry other items of harness all of which must have been worked by hand out of animal hides. He noted also the colour contrast between the leather of the kilt and boots and that of the pouches and harness, realizing as he did so that he was not seeing just a collection of animal skins tacked together for protection or utility but a uniform, with all which a uniform implied.

Kelso himself was tall and thin, topping Warren's five-eleven by at least three inches, but well-muscled. He looked to be in his early thirties and his face and chin were raw as if from constant shaving with a very blunt instrument. His hair, which looked as if it had been cut with a knife, was short and plastered flat against his scalp with something which smelled to high heaven.

Punctiliously, but without the bone-wrenching precision which had gone into the one he had just received, Warren returned the other's salute and said, 'That is correct,

Lieutenant.'

Kelso nodded, then said quickly, 'I have to escort your group to the nearest committee post as fast as possible, sir. I know that you'll have questions to ask, hundreds of them probably, and my job is to answer them. But first we have to get moving . . .'

'What the blazes *is* this place?' somebody behind Kelso burst out harshly. 'We expected a POW dome, with Bug guards and . . . and . . .'

'What about those drums . . .?'

'Committee! What committee . . .?'

Warren cleared his throat irritably and all at once there was silence—except for the drums and distant shouting. He said, 'Go on, Lieutenant.'

Looking suddenly impressed by Warren where before he had been merely respectful, Kelso resumed, 'I will answer all your questions, sir, but first I must get you to the nearest committee post as quickly as possible. There are others out searching for you, too, and it is imperative that we avoid them—I'll explain about that, as well. So if you don't mind, sir, I'd like us to walk as we talk . . .'

The Lieutenant was still standing rigidly to attention, but he kept swaying forward onto the balls of his feet in his urgency to get moving. Warren decided to have pity on him before he fell flat on his face.

'I have yet to meet a Lieutenant who did not know all the answers,' he said drily. 'Very well, Kelso. Lead on.'

With the Lieutenant at his side and the other survivors from *Victorious* crowding their heels in an attempt to stay within earshot they moved off. The pace Kelso set was a fast walk, but each time a drum started on a new message or there was a fresh burst of shouting in the forest he increased it. When a few minutes had gone by without him saying anything, Major Fielding decided that she couldn't wait.

'Why are there others searching for us, Lieutenant?' she said breathlessly. 'Who are they and why must we avoid them . . .?'

Kelso looked quickly towards her, then looked again. The regulation battledress uniform, tight-fitting and designed so that with the addition of a fish-bowl it became a short-duration spacesuit, did nothing for an ageing officer like Warren with his thickening waist-line and tendency towards bow legs, while for officers like Ruth Fielding it did quite a lot. When he replied Kelso was smiling and he spoke loudly enough for everyone to hear.

'To answer that we must first fill in some necessary background details,' he began. 'As you know, for the past sixty-odd years the Bugs and ourselves have been fighting the first interstellar war, and one of the biggest problems on our side was looking after the prisoners of war ...'

CHAPTER TWO

Almost a century earlier, at a time when the culture of Earth had spread to fifty inhabited systems and her colonization programme was still expanding, mankind had made contact with another intelligent race. The name which this race had for itself was a short, clicking sound which could be reproduced only by a few of Earth's top linguists, the difficulties of communication being extreme on both sides. But even so it quickly became evident that the only thing which the aliens had in common with the human race was intelligence.

To the ordinary beings of both species their physical aspect was mutually loathsome, their thought processes mutually incomprehensible and perhaps the correct course would have been to mutually ignore each other's existence. But there were also some extraordinary beings on both sides—beings possessed of high intelligence and an overpowering scientific curiosity who were excited by the possibility of exchanging ideas with another race despite all the difficulties of communication. Beings, in short, who were objective enough to see past an alien and utterly repulsive exterior to the mind within. They could not understand the more subtle workings of each other's minds as yet, but they wanted desperately to go on trying. So instead of being broken off, contact between the two cultures began gradually to widen.

But there was a vast number of people on Earth and on its colony worlds who were not top-flight linguists, nor possessed of the driving scientific curiosity coupled with the fine objectivity of the men who wanted contact—even though these people were themselves kindly and intelligent and as civilized as the next man. It was just that when they saw something which was soft and pallid and crawled wetly on six legs they wanted to stamp on it, and sometimes did before they could stop themselves. The reaction was instinctive, something they couldn't help, and the fact that the thing they wanted to stamp on was nearly as big as themselves only made their reaction that much more violent.

The number of violent incidents grew until, some thirty years after first contact had been made, they reached the proportions of an open war. The people on both sides who had been pleading for greater objectivity when dealing with the aliens were powerless to stop it, but they did retain some influence. Before diplomatic relations were severed completely they reached agreement on certain rules of conduct for the coming war.

It was not to be a total war. Both sides hoped that it would not go on forever, so there was to be no unnecessary slaughter of combatants who were no longer able to defend themselves, or cruelty towards such beings when they were taken prisoner.

In the first two decades of the war the number of major engagements fought increased steadily to a point which would have been considered utterly impossible at the beginning of hostilities, because each side was evenly matched technologically and neither had been capable of realizing the tremendous war potential inherent in a confederation of fifty inhabited systems. And because it was not a war of senseless heroics—the space personnel were much too stable and intelligent for their heroism to be anything other than the cool, calculated sort—there were prisoners taken. During the first five years of the war the number of Bug

13

prisoners taken passed the million mark, and the flood of enemy POWs kept pace with the accelerating tempo of the war. And, plus or minus a few hundred thousand, the Bugs took as many as they lost.

One of the chief reasons for the POW agreement in the first place was the fact that space personnel were extremely valuable people. They represented the cream of the young technical and scientific brains of their respective cultures and they were people which neither side wanted to lose. But the war showed no indication of ending and the few attempts at arranging an exchange of prisoners failed because of already difficult communications problems rendered insuperable by the mounting tensions of war. So the number of prisoners held by each side grew. And grew.

Millions of men and vast quantities of war material were tied up merely in providing for Bug prisoners. The facilities for taking care of them—their food and air required special processing and their housing had to be seen to be believed—became increasingly strained. It quickly reached the point where the whole war effort was being affected by this hampering burden of prisoners, and seemingly there was no solution to the problem . . .

'. . . But twenty-three years ago the Bugs found the solution,' Kelso went on quickly. 'It is a nice, economical and very humane solution. Looked at objectively, its only drawback is that we didn't think of it ourselves . . .'

Above the sound of the Lieutenant's voice and the considerable noise made by his listeners as they blundered through the undergrowth in his wake, Warren could hear the whistles and drums of other searchers growing louder by the minute. He felt angry and afraid and very short of breath, and he wished fervently that Kelso would get to the point of at least letting him know what it was that he was afraid of. But seemingly the Lieutenant intended telling everything in his own way and in proper sequence, and any interjections would serve only to delay the process.

'. . . What they did was to pick one of the worlds in their own sector which was suitable for human colonization,' the Lieutenant rushed on, 'then they dumped fifty thousand or so prisoners onto it with enough supplies, shelters and simple agricultural machinery to enable them to continue

14

as a self-sustaining colony. Other prisoners arrive from time to time, but for the past ten years these new arrivals have not been accompanied by tools or supplies—they don't want us to have any more metal than the bare minimum already supplied by them to begin with, you see. And just in case we did succeed in throwing together a spaceship out of our surplus plough-shares they have a guardship in orbit to keep an eye on things . . .'

The explanation of the Bug POW system would, in ordinary circumstances, have caused great surprise and excited discussion, but the other was pushing the pace so hard that all Warren and the others had breath for was a few incredulous grunts. Even Kelso's breathing was becoming laboured now, but he still continued doggedly with his history lesson.

In words which were becoming more and more emotionally loaded, the Lieutenant described the situation as it had been shortly after the first prisoners had landed. Briefly he detailed the influences and personalities which had brought about the original disagreement among the prison population—a split which had continued to widen so that, when Kelso arrived six years ago, the differences on each side were so strongly held and basic that there was little hope of ever uniting them again. It was generally agreed that a planet-sized POW camp was an ingenious idea and caused the minimum of physical distress to its prisoners. What they could not agree on, and from this disagreement all the later difficulties had stemmed, was that the prison was escape-proof.

'. . . Because there are no domes or guards always in sight, a lot of these people forget that they are in a prison camp!' Kelso went on hotly. 'Not only have they stopped thinking of themselves as prisoners of war, they've forgotten that they are officers and even, judging by the way they act, that there is a war on! They've gone civilian. But on the Committee side, however, we have *not* forgotten that we are prisoners. Or that it is the sworn duty of any officer taken prisoner in time of war to do everything possible to rejoin his unit . . .'

It was at that point that Warren threw his hands out from his sides, palms backwards in a visual order to halt which he did not have the breath to vocalize. The party came to an untidy halt around him. Kelso, whose impetus had carried him several yards ahead, pulled up hurriedly and came trotting back to them. He looked worried and impatient as he waited for Warren to speak.

'These ... these Civilians you talk about,' he got out finally. 'Are they dangerous? Will they eat us, or something? From what you've told me ... they're just ...' He broke off to suck in a lungful of air, then demanded harshly, 'Why the blazes are we *running* ...!'

Kelso did not answer at once. They had reached the base of a long, thinly-wooded slope on whose crest Warren could vaguely make out a high stockade. This would be the Committee post which the Lieutenant had mentioned several times. The civilian searchers were all around them with the nearest group sounding so close that if it hadn't been for the screen of trees they would probably have been in plain sight.

'I ... I can explain all this much better at the post, sir,' Kelso began.

'*Now*, Lieutenant,' said Warren.

'Well, sir,' Kelso said helplessly, 'they won't harm you physically. What they intend is analogous to brain-washing. But what makes it so horribly effective is the fact that most of them don't consider what they're doing to be a form of coercion—they think they are simply being hospitable ...'

Somewhere on their right there was a shout followed by a long blast on a whistle. Immediately all the other whistling and shouting died away so that Warren could hear the swish and crackle of feet running towards them. Kelso swore but did not look round.

Trying desperately to hold Warren's attention he rushed on, 'They begin by welcoming you to the camp, although they've stopped thinking of it as that. Then they over-feed you on their home-cooking, which is particularly effective considering how long you've had to exist on Bug synthesized food. And because it would be too much of a strain on any one farm to take on all of you, you will find yourselves scattered all over the place. You will lose touch with each other and have no way of knowing for sure what each other is doing or thinking. They won't ask you to work at

16

first, but you'll feel obligated for all the hospitality shown you and you will insist on helping out. And they'll keep talking at you all the time.

'As you know, sir,' Kelso went on hurriedly, his voice rising in volume as the sound of running feet approached, 'most highly trained and intelligent people find pleasure in performing menial, non-cerebral jobs. But very soon these pleasant, manual tasks become a way of life. You grow mentally lax and begin to think slow, farmer's thoughts. Soon it would be hard to remember that there is a war going on and that you are an officer with certain obligations and duties to perform . . .'

Three Civilians arrived at that point. They were large, bearded men clad in the same type of animal skins as those which covered the Lieutenant, except that they favoured long, shapeless trousers and an open-at-the-front vest-like garment instead of a kilt. Two of them carried spear-like weapons, the shafts of which were upwards of eight feet long and terminated in a cutting blade whose condition suggested that they might be some kind of farming implement, although the men were not holding them like farming implements. In addition one of them carried a hide-covered drum slung across his back. All three of them looked surprised and angry at the sight of Kelso, and it was the one with the grey beard and the angriest expression who spoke.

'So you found them first, Lieutenant . . .'

'Yes, sir,' Kelso broke in quickly. He was holding the older man's eyes and ignoring the long, dirty but very sharp blades pointed at his midriff, although the tension in the muscles of his neck and shoulders showed the effort it cost him. But his voice was steady as he went on, 'Since I have found them before you did, sir, you will kindly not hinder me or attempt to talk to them while I escort them to the Post.'

'You found them by sheer luck,' the other said furiously. 'And a single, unarmed man isn't capable of protecting maybe thirty people against battlers or anything else! In such circumstances the rule of first contact is ridiculous! I'm ordering you back to the Post, Lieutenant, and you can tell them there that . . .'

While the argument had been going on the three Civilians were joined by six others, three groups of two all of whom were armed with the long spears. When they had been some distance off they had waved and smiled at the new arrivals, but when they saw Kelso their expressions changed. As they crowded around the Lieutenant some of them looked really murderous.

'You're being unfair, sir!' Kelso protested. 'The rule is that the officer who first finds——'

'*Silence!*' the other man shouted, then in a tone only slightly more quiet he went on, 'Rule or no rule, Kelso, I won't allow you to walk off with nearly thirty new arrivals! To make them into troublemakers and unsettle them so that it'll take months or years before we can make them think straight again . . .'

He broke off suddenly to gape at the five men who seemed to have grown out of the grass at their feet. Warren had not seen or heard the men approach and obviously neither had anyone else. They wore the same kilt and harness as did the Lieutenant and they carried weapons resembling cross-bows which they held at the ready. After the first startled look around, Warren's attention was practically dragged back to one of them, a short, heavily-muscled man who at some time had been terribly burned about the head, shoulders and left arm. The injuries must have had deep psychological effects because the eyes which glared out of that terribly disfigured face were more frightening than the face itself. This man held his cross-bow much readier than any of the others.

The five new arrivals did not speak. Apparently they had heard enough of the argument to understand the situation.

Until the arrival of the Civilians Warren had thought that he, too, had understood what was going on. One side was Civilian, comprising officers who accepted their position as hopeless and who were determined to make the best of it. The other side was Committee, obviously taking its name from the escape committee which every POW camp contained, whose members had not given up hope of escape. It was natural to assume that there would be a certain amount of bad feeling between them. The Committee would feel jealous and angry about their happily vegetating

18

colleagues and the so-called Civilians would also be angry because their collective conscience was being continually pricked by the presence and activities of the Committee.

But this was more than simple bad feeling. Kelso and the grey-haired Civilian were glaring at each other, plainly on the point of going to war on each other with their bare hands. The eight civilians armed with spears were spread out facing the five Committeemen, whose weapons were now cocked and aimed. The situation had deteriorated suddenly to the point where a shooting war was likely to break out at any second. And Warren, all too conscious of his position in the undefended centre of things, could not think of a single thing to do or say which might stop it.

CHAPTER THREE

'I think it's nice to have grown men fighting over one,' Ruth Fielding said suddenly. 'It boosts a girl's morale no end.'

It was a completely stupid, fatuous and selfish remark, the sort of remark which might be expected of a certain type of beautiful but dumb female. As well, her expression and tone while making it only strengthened the impression that she was the pretty, dumb and selfish type. But the Committeemen and Civilians had no way of knowing what her rank and position had been aboard *Victorious*, although if they had been thinking straight they would have known that the selfish and stupid personalities were never chosen for space service, no matter how nicely they were wrapped. But these people were not thinking straight, and Fielding had successfully injected a note of ridicule into an extremely grave situation.

Both Kelso and the grey-bearded Civilian turned to gape at her, and the Committeeman with the devastated face pulled back the two stiff masses of scar tissues which were his lips into a smile, although the look in his eyes still made Warren uneasy.

All at once Warren felt angry at himself. He had been mentally asleep on his feet and Fielding had created the diversion which might allow the argument to be resumed with words instead of physical violence, and his self-confidence—or was it his pride?—had taken a beating. The rest was now up to him. He still felt angry and ashamed, but only the anger showed in his voice.

'I seriously doubt, Major Fielding, that they were fighting over you alone,' Warren said harshly. 'And it is *not* nice to have officers fighting among themselves, for any reason whatsoever.

'What I would like to know, gentlemen,' he continued bitingly, with a definite stress laid on the word 'gentlemen', 'is why we are worth fighting over? Do we ourselves have a choice in this matter? Are we property of some kind, a potential slave-labour force perhaps . . .?'

'Oh no, sir . . .!' began Kelso.

'Certainly not!' the Civilian protested, practically shouting him down. 'The very idea is ridiculous! You won't be asked to work until you ask us to give you a job, believe me. Even then the work will be easier, *and* much more useful, than the senseless jobs the Committee would give you . . .'

He paused briefly to snap 'Be quiet, Lieutenant!' at Kelso, who was trying vainly to break in, then went on, 'For example, a few hours after you arrive in the post up there you will begin what is known as De-briefing. You will understand that everyone here, Committeemen and so-called Civilians alike, are curious regarding the progress of the war or the latest news from home. You would expect them to suck you dry of all the news and gossip from our various home planets. But the De-briefing involves much more than this.

'For days on end and for anything up to six hours a day you will be questioned,' he continued grimly, 'with the emphasis on the last few days before your arrival. The interrogation will be conducted under light hypnosis, if you're lucky enough to be a hypnotic subject, and in any event will consist of the same line of questioning repeated over and over. Because the Committee wants to know everything it possibly can about the guardship, and that means everything you saw during trans-shipment and while on the shuttle coming down, together with everything you saw or heard or otherwise noted without knowing that you did so. Without the proper drugs, digging for these trace memories and peripheral images is a long and exhausting business, and what makes it even worse is that it is a complete waste of time . . .!'

'Sir!' Kelso broke in sharply before the other could go on. 'I must insist that you say nothing further to these officers. I found them first and——'

'You found them, yes,' the Civilian snapped back at him, 'but you couldn't have protected them and so your claim to be escorting them is sheer——'

'I can protect them now, sir,' said Kelso in a dangerously quiet voice.

Warren saw the spears and cross-bows being raised again. Two powerful and mutually-opposed ideologies were struggling for his allegiance, it seemed, and he still did not know enough to mediate. All he could do was to attack one of them before they could attack each other.

'Why do you call him "sir", Lieutenant?' Warren asked sharply. 'You've told me that he is a Civilian—someone who, if not actually a deserter, is at very least a person to whom you would not show respect. Yet you call him "sir" and *he* appears to be giving *you* orders . . .!'

'Because he is Fleet-Commander Peters,' Kelso replied, without taking his eyes off the other man. He sounded bitter as well as angry as he went on, 'Because he is the senior officer on the camp. To prisoners like myself who are trying not to forget that we are officers, his rank and position must be respected even though he himself may no longer consider them important . . .'

So this large bearded man dressed in animal skins was a Fleet Commander! In the service an officer of that rank, holding as he did authority over the personnel and facilities necessary for the supply and maintenance of a fleet of anything up to one hundred interstellar ships, was a very potent individual indeed. In the ordinary way a Lieutenant regarded such august beings with much more than mere respect, and Kelso's open contempt towards an officer so vastly his senior angered Warren suddenly. He had to remind himself that this particular Fleet Commander had 'gone civilian' while the Lieutenant had not, and that going civilian in Kelso's book was a very shameful thing to do ...

'I've had enough arguing!' Peters shouted again, his voice squeaking with sheer fury. 'And more than enough, Lieutenant, of your respectful insubordination!' He swung abruptly to face Warren and, lowering his voice slightly, went on, 'I don't have to go down on my knees. As the senior officer on this planet I can order you to come with me ...'

'You can *try*,' Kelso broke in savagely. He turned and began raising his hand in some kind of signal to the waiting Committee bow-men ...

'*Hold it!*'

The sheer volume of his voice made everyone jump and surprised even Warren himself. He must be angrier than he realized, he told himself, to have let go with such a blast of sound. He felt no less angry as he went on, 'A few minutes ago I asked if we had any choice in this matter. I'm still waiting for the answer.'

There was a long, tense silence which was finally broken by the Fleet Commander.

'I don't really want to pull rank in this, you understand,' Peters said in a voice which he was trying to make pleasant. 'All I can do is explain the situation and trust your natural intelligence to guide you correctly. The choice, however, is yours.'

'The rule ...' began Kelso, then shook his head angrily and ended, 'You have a choice, sir, of course.'

'Thank you,' said Warren.

Considering the available information as objectively as possible, Warren thought that there was little to choose between either faction. Kelso had made a strong first impression and his outline of the situation had seemed fair and balanced. On the other hand Peters' contention that the place was escape-proof and that the prisoners should accept that fact was also, on the surface, eminently sane and logical. All the evidence was not yet in, however, and until it was he was reduced to basing his choice on the effect the two

22

people had had on him.

Where Kelso had been concerned, the effect had been good. In a service where practically every operation consisted of several minutes action sandwiched between months of boredom, a very special type of person was required to stand the strain. Warren had spent most of his early life in the service with people of that kind—intelligent, stable, yet enthusiastic people who never seemed to give up. A man who remained clean-shaven when to do so entailed a considerable amount of trouble and, to judge from the many raw patches on his face, pain, might very well be one of those people.

The Fleet Commander, so far as Warren could see, was one of the people who had given up. There were far too many officers like him in the service since the continuing war had forced down the entrance standards. He felt sorry for Peters and a little ashamed of himself for not according the other man the respect due his rank—although he had been so busy trying to keep the two factions from killing each other off that there had been no time for the niceties. And he was sorry also because the Fleet Commander who obviously had been having things all his own way on the planet for a very long time, was in for an unpleasant shock.

'I'll go with the Lieutenant,' said Warren.

The Fleet Commander's teeth came together with an audible click. 'Very well,' he said stiffly. He turned to face the rest of Warren's group and his voice was almost pleading as he went on, 'You officers also have a choice. I trust that some of you will see the sensible course——'

'My officers will do as they're told,' Warren broke in quietly. By way of softening the blow he added, 'Until such times as we have complete information on both sides of this question and are capable of making a final choice, we will stay together and, for the present, go with the Lieutenant.'

Warren could not see the Fleet Commander's expression as Peters wheeled and strode away, snapping orders at his men to disperse them as he went. Within seconds Kelso was asking the Committeemen if they would mind taking up escort position around the new arrivals, and Warren realized suddenly that every single member of the escort outranked the Lieutenant although they obeyed his polite requests at the double. Then as they were once again moving up the slope towards the post, with Kelso fighting hard to keep his grin of triumph within dignified limits, Peters came striding back.

'I'm anxious to hear the latest war news, Lieutenant,' the Commander said in a carefully neutral voice. 'I take it you've no objections to me listening to what they have to say for a while . . .?'

There could be no objection to what on the surface was a completely reasonable request, and Warren began to consider the possibility that he had been a trifle hasty in his estimate of Peters' character—on the present showing the Fleet Commander did *not* appear to be a man who gave up easily . . .

All the way to the post, however, Peters walked at Warren's side without speaking. Several times he looked as if he was about to say something, and on the other side Kelso edged closer so as to be ready to counter it, but he never progressed farther than clearing his throat. Warren took advantage of the silence to examine the layout of the post.

The stockade which surrounded the post was roughly twenty feet high, composed of logs which had been either buried or driven deeply into the ground, and was supported at each corner by four massive trees. The trees had had their lower branches lopped off up to the level of the top of the stockade, and above this the larger branches supported what seemed to be defence or observation platforms linked by a system of catwalks and ladders to the platform which ran along the inside of the stockade. Because the position of its corner posts was governed by nature rather than human design the plan-view of the structure was not quite square and its walls, which had a tendency to curve towards the support of smaller intervening trees, were anything but straight. Entrance was by way of a section of log wall, which dropped open like a draw-bridge and was hauled into position again as they passed through.

Inside the stockade extensive use had again been made of naturally growing trees, which formed the main supports of several large structures and many smaller huts had been built under them, some with extensions into the upper branches. Only the lower branches had been stripped from

24

any of the trees which Warren could see, so that the whole of the stockades' interior was in shadow. He was beginning to realize that the post was a larger and more complex place than he had at first thought, and that it would be practically impossible to spot it from the air.

Or space.

They were shown into a large, log building in which a long table with benches on each side of it occupied one wall while the three other walls were filled with shelves containing hundreds of what seemed to be loose-leaf files. He wondered briefly where all the paper had come from, and added that question to the others on his list. Despite the fact that the log walls and ceiling had been stripped of bark it was still too dim inside the place to make out details.

'When the sun rises a little higher you'll be able to see comfortably,' Kelso explained as he saw Warren peering about. 'The De-briefing can wait until after you've eaten. It's only breakfast, I'm afraid, but there's plenty and it will probably taste like Christmas dinner after the Bug food. But there are a few preliminaries which we can get out of the way while we're waiting . . .' He broke off suddenly as someone called to him from the other side of the room, then said hastily, 'Excuse me, sir. Be right back.'

The buzz of conversation in the room was growing into a muted roar as the Committeemen extended themselves to make the new arrivals feel at home and answer the questions being shot at them from all sides. Warren did not realize that Peters was speaking to him until the Fleet Commander gripped his arm.

'. . . Wondering why a Fleet Commander was out looking for you,' Peters was saying in a quiet, urgent voice, 'and your siding with him was partly due to your feeling of sympathy for the underdog. But Lieutenant Kelso is not an underdog. He leads the Committee just as surely as I lead the so-called Civilians. Six years on the Inner Committee has given him lots of practice in giving orders which sound like polite questions, and similar forms of verbal sleight-of-hand. He uses his superior officers and he'll use you . . .'

Across the room Kelso had ended his conversation with a Committeeman and was pushing his way back through the crowd towards Warren. Peters went on quickly, 'The Committee is in bad shape. It had been steadily losing officers to me for years—its highest ranking officers, which should prove something if you'll stop and think about it. Kelso desperately needs a big stick to wave at me. All he has is a few Flight Colonels and a Flotilla Leader long past retirement, and none of them have the rank or temperament to oppose me directly. I've eaten Colonels before breakfast and——'

Irritated suddenly, Warren said sharply, 'When I've heard the Lieutenant's version I'll listen to yours. Without interruptions and for as long as you like. That's a promise.'

The Fleet Commander seemed to droop, and Warren realized that, despite his powerful physique and hair that was more black than grey, Peters was close to retirement age. When he spoke his voice sounded hurt rather than angry as he said, 'I expect a certain amount of impertinence and insubordination from Committeemen, but new arrivals usually show me the respect due my rank . . .'

'Oh, for Heaven's sake! I didn't mean to sound . . . Yes, Lieutenant?'

'As I was saying, sir,' said Kelso, rejoining them, 'we would like to list the names, ranks and ships of origin of your people. Beginning with yourself, sir.'

'They all came from my ship,' began Warren, then stopped.

'Please go on, Captain,' said Kelso. It was plain that he had already calculated the size of Warren's ship, based on the number of survivors added to the much higher figure of those who had not survived, and the result had impressed him. Doubtless he had already calculated the rank of such a ship's commanding officer.

'I wasn't the Captain,' Warren went on, and saw Kelso look slightly less impressed. But the Lieutenant was still jumping to wrong conclusions, he thought as he turned to face Peters. Almost apologetically he said, 'The ship was the battlecruiser *Victorious*. My flagship. I am Sector-Marshal Warren . . .'

He had done his best to soften the blow, but Peters' expression simply proved to him once again that there was no painless way of telling a man that he is no longer the Boss. Warren turned back to the Lieutenant.

26

Kelso no longer gave the impression of being an intelligent, efficient, eager young officer. His mouth had gone slack and his eyes had an odd, unfocussed look as if he was contemplating some glorious inner vision.

Perhaps it was the vision of a big stick.

CHAPTER FOUR

It wasn't that he was being forced to do anything, Warren thought dourly as he mounted to the roof of the administration hut and began the long climb to the main observation platform; there wasn't a single Committeeman on the post who wouldn't jump to his bidding. Yet for the past three weeks he had done all the things which had been required of him. Or was it perhaps that he was doing all the things which Kelso required of him . . .?

His interrogation during De-briefing had been long and painfully thorough. After Peters' remarks on that subject Warren had expected Kelso to waive, or at least tone down, that part of the business. But the Lieutenant had told him that they had no wish to make a liar out of the Fleet Commander, and that the data gathered during De-briefing was really of vital importance—so much so that they would risk the displeasure of even a Sector Marshal rather than omit a single hour of questioning.

And with the others of his party he had submitted to wearing fatigues. There had been no direct pressure involved in this, it was simply that the climate made wearing them more comfortable—especially during drills and weapon practice when the kilt gave complete freedom of movement. But the Committeemen's reason for wearing fatigues, they had told him, was to keep the light-weight spacesuits in operable condition against the time when they would be needed to take the Bug guardship.

When they took the guardship, Warren had noted, never *if* . . .

From all over the Post the sound of voices drifted up to him as he climbed. Some were quiet, some excited and many of them were interspersed with shouts of laughter. The merriment was probably coming from the group receiving instruction in the handling of a cross-bow, and another sound like a flock of woodpeckers labouring not quite in unison originated from the group doing elementary Communications on sticks and tree trunks before being turned loose on the signal drums.

He had submitted to and accepted many things, one of the most difficult being his replacement of Peters as senior camp officer. Because of his rank Warren had had no choice in the matter, but it had shaken him a little to find himself the supreme authority on a planet containing upwards of half a million prisoners a few hours after landing on it. But not seriously, because Warren was accustomed to wielding such authority. What did bother him was Kelso's assumption that he would automatically head the Escape Committee. The Lieutenant was forcing matters by putting Warren in the position of heading a project which he had not yet finally agreed to join, and he wanted to have a long, hard think about it before the meeting of the Inner Committee which Kelso had called for that afternoon.

And while he was thinking he did not want eager young Committeemen jogging his mental elbow, which was his reason for climbing to the highest observation platform on the Post. That was why, when he was negotiating the final ladder and the sound of voices drifted down to him, he felt considerably annoyed.

'. . . At night or during overcast condition,' one of the voices was saying, 'we use signal drums. A big drum slung at this height, provided the wind is in the right direction, has about the same range as the heliograph, which is this contraption here. The sighting arrangement is accurate although we haven't had much luck with silvering our mirrors.'

'How about the telescope?' a female voice asked, and Warren recognized it as Ruth Fielding's. 'Big for a refractor, isn't it?'

28

'That's for keeping tabs on the guardship,' the first voice replied. 'The clockwork mechanism is mostly wood, and provided a breeze isn't moving the whole tree-top through several degrees of arc and seeing is good, we can keep it centred pretty well. But chromatic aberration is fierce—most of the time the ship looks like some sort of Christmas tree. There's enough definition, though, to let us know when another ship joins it in orbit or the shuttle leaves to land more prisoners.'

The words were apologetic but the tone was not, Warren thought. It was the voice of a person justifiably proud of having accomplished much with practically nothing. It went on, 'The glass comes from the coast fifty miles north of here. Maybe it's the wrong kind of sand, or maybe we're just lousy glass-makers, but we're experimenting with . . .'

The voice stopped suddenly and a Committeeman with a Major's insignia picked out on his harness was looking down at Warren. The Major gave him a hand up, saluted and stood to attention.

'Thank you,' said Warren, then; 'I want to speak to Major Fielding. Alone, if you don't mind.'

That removed the Committeeman from the scene, but telling Fielding to scat would have to be managed a little more tactfully—if he decided to send her away at all. It might be a good idea to discuss some of the aspects of his problem with a psychologist.

'Well, Ruth,' he said, ducking under the mass of cordage which radiated from the telescope mount and coming to within a comfortable talking distance. 'What is your opinion of this place? Personal and professional, that is.'

His use of the first name signified just two things, that the officer currently being addressed was not in his bad books and that he wished to conduct the ensuing conversation without the usual hampering load of 'Yes, sirs.'

'Good morning, sir,' said Fielding. She had been about to salute but on realizing that this was to be an informal discussion she smoothly grabbed an overhanging rope instead. The rope gave with her and high above them a branch heavy with leaves moved aside, allowing a shaft of sunlight to strike the heliograph mounting behind her. Fielding took her hand away quickly and the leafy camouflage rustled

29

back into place. She laughed.

'Personally I like it,' she said enthusiastically. 'I think we all like it, and a lot of us have had much worse times and enjoyed ourselves a whole lot less when home on leave—although that isn't saying much since our home planets are pretty grim places these days. And since that battleship on legs tried to climb the stockade last week, nobody objects to being confined to the Post, until they learn how to use a cross-bow properly.'

'Then I have an objection,' Fielding replied seriously. 'Just *look* at me . . .!'

Fatigues, female officers for the use of, consisted of a sleeveless hide shirt without shape and shorts which were too baggy and too long. Wearing them Fielding was still a good-looking girl, but after the manner of a Cinderella before the transformation scene. Warren smiled.

'This is a professional objection?' he asked drily.

'Yes, sir,' said Fielding, still seriously. 'It points up the fact that this is a man's world. Oh, I know that the Committee-men could not be more polite in their treatment of us. But there's a tenseness about it—they act almost as if they were boys out on their first date, which is ridiculous since there must be as many female officers on the planet as there are males. Also, they never discuss anything of real importance with any of the girls, and the jobs we're given are all in the third leg category—mere time passers! So far none of our girls have noticed this, but it seems obvious to me that female officers are *not* wanted on the Escape Committee!'

'Go on,' said Warren quietly.

Fielding looked surprised, as if she had expected a more violent reaction than this, then she continued, 'From a few things I've heard and from data I've gathered from the files—I was on a paper-cutting detail for a week—the situation appears to me to be something like this . . .'

According to Fielding the Committee considered women to be a bad risk. Their basic drives—the maternal instinct, the need for security and so on—pre-disposed them towards the Civilian philosophy, this being proved by the fact that practically every unattached female officer went civilian during the first six months, and that even the husband and wife combinations rarely lasted longer. This caused a heavy surplus of women in the Civilian camp, so that the ones who had not been fortunate enough to find Civilian husbands had to do their best to snare, and convert to Civilian ideas, one of the Committeemen.

This was encouraged in every way possible by the Fleet Commander, and the result was a further erosion of the Committee ranks in addition to the losses caused by the usual propaganda methods. As things were, Peters would have been statistically certain of getting two thirds of the newly arrived officers if one of them had not happened to outrank him. Peters was winning, and without having to work really hard at it . . .

'. . . But the ones who stay in the Committee are tough,' Fielding went on. 'They are not misogynists exactly, but their urges in that direction have been pretty thoroughly sublimated to the idea of Escape. They have found that, generally speaking, females can't be trusted. That the few who do honestly want to stay and work for the Committee only cause trouble anyway, and that it is better to discourage them gently from the start.

'And I do mean gently,' she added quickly. 'We couldn't possibly take offence at anything they've said or done. But the situation here—on the planet as a whole, not just in the Post—is psychologically unstable. Dangerous even.

'Professionally,' she added, 'I don't like it.'

In the silence which followed, Warren thought very hard. Fielding's outline of what, to her, seemed a dangerous and unstable situation was fairly accurate, but the truth was that it was much more serious than she realized. Warren also had access to files, the files restricted to members of the Inner Committee, and he did not like the situation either. And he was aware, too, that Kelso was pushing him. Warren did not mind that so long as he was being pushed in the direction he wanted to go, and he had climbed up here to try to decide exactly which direction it was that he intended to take. But now, and without him having the chance to hear Peters' side of it, the decision was being forced upon him.

A burst of laughter drifted up to him, followed by the sound of someone getting a good-natured bawling out for missing the target and losing cross-bow bolts in the long grass. It was very hard just then for him to think of these pleasant, efficient and enthusiastic young Committeemen as being a threat.

'Would you like to help found a dynasty?' he asked Fielding suddenly.

Fielding's face went red. 'Are you *serious*?' she said. Then realizing that her tone could have given offence on several levels of meaning she altered it subtly so that the question sounded mildly improbable instead of utterly ridiculous, and repeated, '*Are* you serious, sir?'

Warren did not reply at once. He was thinking that the Committee as it now stood was something of an *elite* corps, that the officers who had remained in it had survived in spite of extreme psychological pressures, and that to do so they must be little short of fanatical in their devotion to what they considered was their duty. It had also occurred to Warren that out of a prison population of half a million widely scattered and disorganized farmers they represented a well-disciplined and relatively mobile force of something like twenty thousand, and that if Peters had his own way much longer and succeeded in trimming their numbers even further so that they themselves realized that an escape was no longer possible, then the Fleet Commander and the Civilians he represented would be in very serious trouble indeed.

At present they were something less than respectful towards senior officers who did not share their ideas, and it would only be a short step to the point where a further reduced and hence even more fanatical ex-Escape Committee took over the place by force.

Such a military dictatorship might not be too bad, Warren thought, except that civil war must follow inevitably and soon. Far too many of the Committee officers were of equal rank, and there was bound to be furious disagreement as to who would be Boss. All these things, although distant in time, were not only probable but virtual certainties, and Warren had been trying for more than a week to devise a plan which would put this probability into the impossible class. Founding a dynasty—remaining in his present position, that was, consolidating it and passing his ideas as well as his supreme authority on to his descendants—was a nice

32

if rather fanciful idea. But even the stability of a monarchy was not always certain and, judging by Fielding's first reaction to the suggestion and bearing in mind the fact that she was a doctor as well as a psychologist, the idea might be physiologically impossible anyway.

Of one thing he was sure, however. The Fleet Commander was ultimately on the losing side no matter which choice Warren made. Even if he should side with Peters and use his considerable weight of authority against the Committee, he would succeed in further reducing their numbers but at the cost of making them a more closely-knit and fanatical group. No matter how he looked at it the situation was a potentially dangerous one which must sooner or later lead to a shooting war.

Warren sighed, bringing his mind back from a probably disastrous future to a present which was, literally, full of laughter, sunshine and excitement. Smiling, he said, 'Relax, Doctor. The question was purely rhetorical.'

So far as Warren could see there was only one solution to his problem. He must join the Escape Committee.

And escape.

CHAPTER FIVE

Shortly after the meeting began the rain started and the light which made its way through the natural camouflage and into the administration hut became so dim that Warren could barely make out the faces of the four other officers around the table. Proceedings were held up while Kelso lit the lamps and positioned their reflectors so as to direct all the available light onto the map which had been attached, in sections, to the largest clear area of wall.

Nearly eight feet high and twenty long, the map showed the prison planet in Mercator projection. A large, elongated diamond-shaped continent was centred on the equator and was connected to a smaller continent, triangular in shape and also lying on the equator, by a long chain of islands. The large continent, the islands and the two indistinct land masses at each pole were little more than outlines, but the smaller continent was shown in considerable detail.

Major Hynds, who was chief of the Intelligence sub-committee, spoke as Kelso resumed his seat.

'As you will have already guessed, sir,' he said, 'the smaller continent is the one occupied by the prisoners. From data gathered by Committee exploration parties and from the observations of people lucky enough to be near a port on the shuttle coming down we have obtained a fairly accurate idea of this continent's topology. Everything else on the map, however, was pieced together from the interrogation of the few officers who were able to view the planet from the guardship's orbit. Because of the acute angle of observation, the unfortunate fact that continental outlines have a habit of being obscured by cloud and because some people just have not got the ability to draw what they remember seeing, this must be considered unreliable.'

Hynds was a small, lightly-built man with a tendency towards sarcasm. He wore glasses which had been repaired so many times that their nose- and ear-pieces were shapeless blobs of paper and gum. He steadied them with a finger and thumb while he talked, using the other hand as a pointer.

The positions of Committee posts were marked by red feathers, farms and farming villages by green, Hynds went on to explain, with the roads connecting these civilian installations shown in black. Committeemen used these roads extensively, since they had been instrumental in building most of them, but great pains were taken to ensure that the Civilian road system was not linked, even by a forest path, to the Posts. The existence of the camouflaged Posts was not known to the enemy, as was proved by the fact that this one had been built within a few miles of a favourite landing spot.

The two black triangles were ore-bearing mountains, it having been found that the widely-dispersed ore effectively screened the small masses of refined metal underlying it from the guardship's detectors. These were the sites of the

34

Committee smelting plants and advanced training units, the existence of which was not known even to the Civilians.

So the movement was already going underground, in both senses of the word, Warren thought drily. He had been right to join them because he certainly could not have beaten them. Not completely.

'You mentioned advanced training units,' Warren broke in suddenly. 'Would you expand on that, please.'

'That is Major Hutton's department, sir,' said Hynds, seating himself and glancing towards the officer beside him.

The table jerked and made scraping noises against the floor as Hutton got to his feet. He was an enormous man, fantastically muscled and with a mat of chest hair so thick that in places it concealed the straps of his harness, But his expression was intelligent, apologetic and eager to please, and Warren was reminded of a good-natured and well-meaning bull to whom the whole world was a china shop. When he spoke his voice was barely audible, as if it, like his tremendous body, had also to be kept constantly in check.

'As you can understand, sir,' Hutton murmured, 'a large amount of preparatory work is necessary before the escape plan can be put into effect. Experiments with the extraction and processing of metallic ores, which present certain difficulties considering the limited facilities at our disposal and the need for concealing the work. We have teams working on glass-blowing, chemical explosives, air liquifaction and storage problems and so on. Then there is the work on the guardship mock-up, and on the dummy itself.

'We need men to build and maintain the wood-burning steam engines used for the heavy jobs,' Hutton went on quietly, 'a steam engine being the best our machine shops are capable of producing at present. Even if we could make one, the ignition of an internal combustion engine might be picked up by Bug instruments, so steam is safer—although we've drilled successfully for oil, which is used mainly for lighting the tunnels and labs. In actual fact, however, a machine shop is little more than a mediaeval smithy ...'

'Major Hutton is being over-modest, sir,' Kelso put in quickly. 'Despite the handicaps, his Technical and Research section is farther advanced in its part of the plan than any of the others.'

35

'Maybe so,' Hutton returned, his voice rising, almost to conversational level and becoming something less than apologetic, 'but it is my job to train a certain number of officers for maintenance and support duties and I'm not getting enough of them, nor am I getting the right kind of men. The people sent me are the ones Hynds considers least likely to go Civilian, not officers whose previous specialities best suit them for the work in hand ...!'

'Nonsense, sir!' Hynds protested, glaring at Hutton. 'I've sent him every chemist and metallurgist I could scrape up. What does he want me to do, send him Civilians ...?'

Hutton was staring at the table top, looking more sullen than angry. Hynds was trying to murder him with his eyes and Kelso was looking from one to the other, obviously annoyed at the impression his two superior officers had created. The other officer at the table, Major Sloan showed no perceptible reaction. Subtle variations of expression were impossible for his ruined face.

'Since I lack data on this subject,' Warren said sternly to the two Majors, 'my comments at this time would be valueless. However, an escape plan has been mentioned several times. What exactly does it involve and when do you propose putting it into effect?'

He looked at Kelso.

'There have been a number of plans submitted to the Escape Committee from time to time,' the Lieutenant said brightly, trying to dispel the unpleasantness of a few minutes previously, 'the custom being to label them with the names of their originators. There was the Fitzgerald Plan, which was very well detailed and called for an attack on the guardship with two-man, chemically powered rockets. Quite apart from the fact that the Bugs would be unlikely to stand around doing nothing while we developed the technology to build the ships, the plan was not feasible because of the length of time required in the preparatory stages.

'The plan which was adopted,' Kelso went on, his tone becoming more serious, 'was the one put forward by Flotilla-Leader Anderson ...'

Anderson had begun by accepting the fact that the only practical way of getting off the planet was to use a Bug ship, his idea being to lure the shuttle rocket to the surface

36

at a predetermined point and in such circumstances that the prisoners would be able to capture it. With the shuttle in their hands it should be possible to effect the capture of the guardship itself, an obsolete battlewagon which was easily capable of transporting anything up to one thousand ex-POWs' to an Earth base, where the news of the existence and position of the planet could be given to the proper authorities.

It was a simple, daring plan which at practically every stage was packed with things which could go wrong. But Anderson had been able to eliminate enough of the uncertainties so that it would be workable with just the average amount of good luck instead of a multiple chain of miracles.

The bait which would lure down the Bug ferryship would be a metal dummy of a crash-landed enemy reconnaissance vessel, assembled during a time when the guardship's orbit kept it below the horizon, from parts prefabricated and hidden in indetectable caches. Then to make sure that the guardship simply did not bomb his mock-up as they had bombed earlier collections of metal on the surface, carefully positioned fires would be started in the surrounding vegetation to make it plainly obvious to the guardship that a vessel had crash-landed, a vessel which on closer inspection would show to be one of their own scoutships.

By displaying signs of life from the dummy ship and perhaps going to the extent of seeming to attack it with human prisoners, it was hoped to bring the Bug shuttle down on a rescue mission . . .

Listening to Kelso's low, impassioned voice as he went on to describe the work already done on the plan, Warren felt excited in spite of himself, and suddenly he found himself wanting to re-examine his motives for doing what he had done.

Granted that his chief reason for joining the Committee had been to try to effect an escape, that being the only sure way of avoiding dissension, civil war and an ultimate descent into near-savagery. This did not mean, however, that the Committee were war-mongers or murderers at the present time—far from it. The people on the Committee side were a group of able, intelligent and resourceful officers who had maintained and even increased their enthusiasm despite years of constantly mounting opposition and steadily dwindling numbers, and Warren was beginning to admire them.

Another reason, and one which he had not yet made public, was that the war was going very badly for the human side and that the Earth forces were urgently in need of the officers who were rapidly going to seed on this prison planet. At one time an *elite* corps which accepted only the best, the space service was scraping the bottom of the personnel barrel these days for crew. This was something Warren knew from bitter personal experience.

And yet another reason, a purely selfish one this time, was that Warren badly wanted to have officers serving under him again who refused to believe that they were beaten, or that anything was impossible . . .

All at once he became aware that he had missed a lot of what the Lieutenant had been saying, and that Kelso's customary tone of enthusiasm had changed to one of anger and frustration—the combination of emotions which were, apparently, the nearest Committeemen came to feeling despair.

'. . . But the most galling fact of all,' the Lieutenant went on bitterly, 'is that the plan had already been initiated years before any of the officers here had arrived! When I came there were half a dozen concealed observation posts in operation close to the most likely landing areas. The first smelter was working and the maximum safe quantity of metal which could be collected in one spot, both on the surface and buried at various depths underground, had been ascertained experimentally—the experiment usually consisting of increasing the quantity until the Bugs noticed and dropped a couple of tons of old-fashioned H.E. on it. The special commando which were to take the Bug shuttle and later the guardship were already being trained, together with the Supply and Intelligence groups to support them. By this time we should have been off this planet, or at least have made a damned good try at getting off it!'

Kelso took a deep breath and exhaled it angrily through his nose, then he went on, 'Instead the plan has been hampered and sabotaged at every turn. We on the Committee, who are trying to retain our traditions and self-respect and discipline as officers, are very often forced to obey people we consider our superiors but who are at heart merely people who have given up and who want everyone else to give up, too, so that their consciences can get together and call black white. The result is that we've been forced to conceal nearly everything we do from fellow officers who by rights should be giving us the fullest co-operation.

'At the present rate of progress, sir,' Kelso ended hotly, 'we'll be lucky if we can make the attempt fifteen or twenty years from now!'

Further along the table Hutton and Sloan, the officer whose speciality was assault training, nodded their agreement. Major Hynds, still holding onto his spectacles as he turned to face Warren, said, 'A conservative estimate, sir, but based on the assumption that we do not lose any more of our officers to the Civilians . . .'

He stopped speaking as one of the drums in the tree above them began rattling out the signal, three times repeated, which summoned the night guard to their stations and simultaneously announced 'Lights Out' to everyone else. Like puppets controlled by a single string the four officers at the table pushed back their chairs and rose to their feet.

'Sit down,' said Warren.

He did not raise his voice, but quite a lot of Kelso's anger and frustration seemed to have rubbed off on him and Warren made no attempt to conceal the fact. At the same time he had no intention of allowing his anger to develop into an uncontrolled outburst of fury, because he knew that a leader who was subject to fits of temper might inspire fear in his subordinates rather than confidence and Warren wanted to inspire both. These Committeemen wanted a leader, and as Warren began to speak he did everything possible short of flaying them with whips to give them the idea that they had acquired one who could drive as well as lead.

To begin with he was merely bitingly sarcastic regarding officers who had practically conditioned themselves to jump when drums banged or whistles blew, going on to suggest that it was this too-rigid insistence on discipline which was one reason for the continuing loss of Committeemen to Peters' Civilians, and that if the present trend continued, the Escape Committee would become a hard core of performing monkeys who did things when somebody made a noise and remained at attention at all other times.

Without altering his scathing tone of voice in the slightest his remarks veered gradually from the derogatory to the constructive.

He was deeply concerned over the dwindling numbers of the Escape Committee, he told them. Not only must this steady erosion cease but they must win back a large proportion of these so-called deserters, and every possible method of influencing them must be explored ranging from subtle psychology to outright blackmail if necessary. The shortage of manpower was the basic reason why the plan had never gotten off the ground, in both senses of the word, and this was a problem which must be, and would be solved.

And taking all the foregoing as read, he now required a breakdown into previous specialities and present aptitudes of all prisoners, also the minimum numbers and training needed by these officers to allow the four sub-committees represented here to bring the Anderson Plan to complete readiness in a reasonable time.

Fifteen years was *not* a reasonable time, Warren insisted. He suggested an absolute top limit of three years . . .

'. . . According to Lieutenant Kelso, most of the data we need is available on this Post,' Warren concluded, his tone becoming slightly more friendly, 'and I intend going into it fully with you now. So I am afraid, gentlemen, that the lights will not go out in this building, nor will any of you see your bunks, until together we have set a date for the Escape . . .'

The faces along the table looked chastened in varying degrees by the tongue-lashing which had gone before and startled by his bombshell regarding the setting of the escape date. But these emotions gave way quickly to a steadily mounting excitement which was reflected in shining eyes and lips which were trying hard not to smile. There was no incredulity, no objections, no verbal response of any kind, and Warren knew suddenly that these officers did not have to be driven to do their duty and he should have realized that. Watching them he felt the warm, tingling contagion of their excitement again and all at once he wanted to praise and compliment them for what they were and for the glorious and well-nigh impossible thing they were trying to do. But a Sector Marshal did not pay such compliments to junior officers, even when they were deserved. It was very bad for discipline.

Instead he allowed his manner to thaw some more and said, 'I'm a reasonable man, however. At this time I won't insist on setting the hour . . .'

CHAPTER SIX

It was E-Day minus one thousand and thirty-three and the officers on the Post were beginning not to smile self-consciously when they referred to it in that way, and they did not smile at all if they were discussing it with the Sector Marshal.

Warren had taken over the main administration building as his headquarters, partitioning off one corner of the big room into an office and sleeping quarters. The office partition, which had a hole in the roof to accommodate the ladder going to the communications platform, was so placed that all maps, records, dossiers, Post personnel, messages via drum or heliograph and an appreciable quantity of rain reached him with the minimum of delay. The office also gave an illusion of privacy, although the hide walls were so thin that every word carried clearly to the men and women he had staffing the outer room.

Present for their regular morning meeting were Major Sloan, the officer in charge of Supply and Assault Training, Major Hynds of Intelligence and Lieutenant Kelso whose job was Co-ordination, Major Hutton having returned to his subterranean smithy two weeks previously, taking with him seven officers from *Victorious* whose training, past hobbies and/or present enthusiasm made them useful to him.

When the salutes had been exchanged and the men stood at ease, Warren said briskly, 'It goes without saying that our work in the past has been seriously hampered by the fact that the so-called Civilians outranked the officers on the Committee. And that the same situation occurs within the Committee in that officers who possess ability often do not possess the rank which should go with it. In order to act effectively such officers must employ flattery and cajolery and similar verbal stratagems, and this you will admit is a gross waste of time and ability.

'While my rank gives me wide powers in the matter of promoting able officers serving under me,' Warren continued, 'I am forbidden to exercise this power while held prisoner of war. But this does not mean that I cannot employ the principles of general staff command and relay my orders through junior officers, delegating such authority as seems necessary. This being so, the present heads of subcommittees are hereby appointed to my Staff and Lieutenant Kelso, because of his recognized ability to handle people nominally his superior, will become my personal aide . . .'

Warren paused to note their reactions. Kelso and Hynds were grinning hugely and Sloan was showing more teeth than usual. They all had an anticipatory gleam in their eyes as if mentally rehearsing what they would say the next time they met the Fleet Commander or any other high-ranking Civilian. In short, the reaction was as expected.

Tapping the uneven wood of his desk for emphasis, Warren resumed sternly, 'As officers on my Staff you will accord your seniors, whether Committee or otherwise, the respect due their rank. You will pass on my orders but you will not throw my weight around. You will be polite and respectful at all times, but you will not accept no as an answer at any time . . . !'

More than any other single factor, the success of the Anderson Plan hinged on the presence in the escape area of a tremendous volume of manpower, every single unit of which would have to be trained and rehearsed in their movements beyond any possible chance of error. Hutton's section could be counted on to prepare the dummy ship sections and train the technical support groups, while Hynds and Sloan took care of communications and the assault. But transporting the metal sections to the escape area and assembling them all within the severely limited time during which the guardship's orbit took it below the horizon, was an operation far beyond the capability of the Committee at its present strength.

Their first concern, therefore, must be to gain recruits.

As Warren saw it, the reasons for an officer leaving the Committee were three-fold. Serving with the Committee was a hard life, the hardship was pointless since they had come to believe the Committee's objective impossible of fulfillment, and since they were unable to take part in the war the sensible course seemed to be to enjoy their enforced peace.

From his study of the available data, however, Warren went on to explain, he was pretty sure that the consciences of these officers gave them considerable trouble—a significant indication being the touchy way most of them reacted to being called Civilians. So if it could be shown that the escape plan was more than just a pipe dream, and if certain of the rules which hitherto had been necessary for Committee membership were to be relaxed somewhat, Warren was certain that many of the so-called deserters could be persuaded to rejoin.

The first step would be for the Committee to wipe out of its collective mind the word 'Civilian'. All *non-Committee* officers would be treated with respect, and the respect should be in no way diminished merely because the officer held different opinions from oneself. They must be made to feel needed and important—that their co-operation was vital to the success of the plan, which was in fact the case. Even partial co-operation, part-time membership of the Committee, would be welcomed. The main thing was to instil the idea into the prisoners' minds that the escape was possible, *that it would take place . . . !*

'. . . With that fact generally accepted,' Warren continued, 'we will be in a position to bring more direct pressure to bear ... Yes, Lieutenant?'

At the news that he was to be Warren's aide, a position which in effect made him second-in-command and chief advisor to the Marshal, Kelso's face had displayed a look of almost wolfish pleasure. But as Warren had elaborated on his plans the Lieutenant had become increasingly restive. Something was definitely bothering him.

'Security, sir,' he burst out, then hesitated. 'You shouldn't discuss details with ... with ...' He nodded violently towards the partition. 'There are women out there, sir!'

Warren toyed for a few seconds with a selection of sarcastic retorts, then pushed them reluctantly aside. He said, 'Explain yourself, please.'

Kelso opened with some muttered remarks to the effect that he approved of women in general and of the surviving female officers from *Victorious* in particular, and that they had been very efficient in chasing up Committee records and progress reports for the Marshal. Nonetheless, the unpleasant fact had to be faced that women on the Escape Committee had been demonstrated time and time again that they were a bad risk. Kelso went on to cite instances, and Major Hynds nodded agreement each time. For the best interests of the movement, the Lieutenant insisted all female officers should be gotten rid of as quickly as possible, because girls were born to be civilians ...

'Get them off the Post!' Major Sloan broke in suddenly. The bass rumble of his voice—like a distant volcano, Warren thought; deep, powerful and with overtones of instability—must have carried much farther than the outer office. 'And not politely, either! The longer they stay the more they unsettle the men. They're soft and they make the men soft. Get rid of them!'

There was a tense silence during which nobody looked at anybody else and even the noises from the outer office seemed to stop. Warren, keeping his face expressionless, regarded the big wall map and tried to decide whether to squelch this Major Sloan now or later, or at all. He knew that normally Sloan did not have much to say for himself. He was responsible for non-technical field training, road and bridge construction, procurement of food and skins by hunting parties or through trading with the farms, and a

44

host of subsidiary jobs. In these duties the Major was quietly and almost fanatically efficient, and this was one of the two reasons which made Warren inclined to make allowances for a certain lack of charm in the man.

The other reason was that on the day of his arrival the Major had not run quickly enough when the Bug shuttle had begun to take off. The burns he had received were of such severity that by rights he should have died from shock. But Major Sloan had been and was an unusually strong man and he had survived despite the absence of proper medical facilities—the Bugs did not supply prisoners with drugs or instruments, so that home-grown and relatively ineffective substitutes had been used in an attempt to relieve his pain. But for nearly two days the Major had screamed, Warren had been told by a Committeeman who still looked sick at the memory of it, and for three weeks after that he had been unable to talk coherently because of the pain. Eventually, however, his body had healed itself although it was plain to anyone who spoke to the Major that the process had stopped short at his mind.

Warren sighed inwardly and was about to speak when Hynds forestalled him.

'I agree with the Major, sir. And if I had as much trouble with this particular problem as he has had, my language might be even stronger . . .'

Obviously Hynds had been expecting Warren to blow up over Sloan's outburst and he was trying desperately to head the Marshal off, not by apologizing for the Major but by agreeing with him. As quickly, and as quietly as he could, Hynds went on, '. . . The desertion of female officers to the Civilians is a statistical certainty and we have been simply hastening the process in various subtle ways. Their uniforms for instance, and paper-making. You know that we get paper—sheets of thin, fine-textured wood, actually—fairly easily. One of the trees here, when the sections of the trunk are boiled to remove the resin, comes apart at the growth rings. The Committee couldn't exist without this paper, but getting it is a horribly messy job and one definitely not suited to women—the gum stains their hands and if it gets in their hair . . .'

'It's necessary and valuable work,' Lieutenant Kelso said,

45

catching the conversational ball neatly, 'and when they've had enough of it we don't just kick them out. They go to Andersonstown, on the coast. That's a large Civilian farming community which grew up around the post responsible for fishing the bay and nearby river . . .'

It had been at a time when relations between the Committee and Civilians had been more cordial that the post had been set up, Kelso went on to explain, and the idea had been to trade fish as well as meat and protection against marauding battlers for grain, fruit and similar necessities. But the scheme had backfired badly so far as the Committee was concerned.

In those days the Civilians had been allowed to build farms very close to the Committee Posts, and they had done so. And because even in those days there were a lot more females than there were male Civilians, and these female officers naturally refused to share a husband with another woman, the only hope they had of getting a husband was to subvert a Committeeman. This they had done to such good effect that the post had had an almost complete turnover of personnel every year. Flotilla-Leader Anderson, the Anderson whose plan had been adopted for the escape and who had been the commanding officer of the post in question, had given the settlement its name when he had gone Civilian. Gradually, the surplus females from all over the continent had moved to Andersons town and the Post had lost more and more of its male officers until eventually the Committee had withdrawn all males from the Post.

'. . . Now it is manned, if you can call it that, entirely by female officers,' Kelso concluded, grinning. 'Girls who can't find Civilian husbands or who don't want to leave the Committee for some other reason. They do some very useful work as well as being a very disturbing influence on the Civilian farmers in the area.'

As the Lieutenant stopped talking Warren found himself thinking about these highly-trained and intelligent girls who, although they might be as eager to get off the planet as anyone on the Committee, were denied the chance to contribute towards the escape. It was not anger at Sloan's insubordination or at the attempts of the other two to cover for the Major which hardened Warren's voice when

46

he spoke.

'Your comments on this matter are appreciated, gentlemen,' he said, 'although they in no way alter the decision which I have already made regarding this problem.

'A point which you don't seem to grasp,' he went on grimly, 'is that the survivors of *Victorious*, because it was a tactical command ship, are very special people compared with the usual run of serving officers today. I don't want to see any single one of them, male or female, going Civilian! And a second point is that fifteen or twenty years ago, at the time when most of the people here were taken prisoner, these same officers would not have been considered special at all. Which shows you how drastically the standards of the service have been lowered and how vitally important it is for the officers on this planet to be returned to active service—such an event would almost certainly bring about the end of the war in our favour! It should also explain why I want every prisoner, regardless of sex, to be serving on or to be in some way associated with the Escape Committee.

'With this in mind,' he continued almost gently, 'I have appointed Major Fielding, the psychologist and medical officer from *Victorious*, to the Staff.'

Warren paused, regarding the suddenly stricken faces staring down at him, then he smiled.

'Please don't look as if your best friends had just died,' he said chidingly. 'Our half of the human race has managed to co-exist with the females of the species, peacefully on the whole if not with complete understanding, for several millenia. I am simply asking the members of the Escape Committee to do the same for three short years . . .'

CHAPTER SEVEN

Next day Warren dispatched Kelso, Hynds and two other responsible officers from the Post on a good-will mission to the surrounding farms and settlements, at the same time signalling the other posts to send out as many officers as could be spared with similar instructions. These orders were designed to show the so-called Civilians that a major change of policy had taken place within the Committee, and while explaining the ramifications of this change the visiting Committeemen were to bend every effort to be frank, friendly and helpful to the farmers—especially in the matter of doing odd jobs of construction and maintenance and in putting down marauding battlers. They were also ordered to show all due respect towards these fellow officers, being particularly careful to avoid dumb insolence or sarcasm, and on no account were they to refer to these non-Committee officers as Civilians—they were to refrain from even thinking of them as such. These non-Committeemen and women were to be regarded simply as imprisoned officers who on a certain day already fixed in the not too distant future would be breaking out of their prison, and that any assistance they felt like giving, whether it was full-time service with the Committee or an hour or so a day on preparatory work, would be very much appreciated . . .

Already drafted were a series of follow-up orders in increasingly firm language, which would not go out until the present tension between the two factions had eased considerably and the preparations for the Escape were far advanced, one of which stated, 'Owing to the necessity of gathering up-to-date information on the disposition of friendly and enemy forces prior to the Escape, all officers are asked to interrogate new arrivals regarding these matters or, if they feel unable to execute this duty with the required efficiency, to escort them to the nearest Post without delay.'

To Ruth Fielding he said, 'You've been appointed to the Staff because I need a good psychologist who can evaluate the overall situation here and help me guide it in the direction I think it must go, and who is also capable of seeing it from the woman's angle. We don't really need the help of *every* officer on the planet, but the ones we *do* want—the chemists, metallurgists and engineers that Hutton is screaming for—all seem to have married or gone civ ... Oops, sorry, I mean they have left the Committee. To get these men, it seems to me, we must first interest their wives in the project.

'This might be accomplished,' he went on, 'by you mentioning at some length the absence of civilized amenities here, such as decent feminine clothing, make-up and whatever else it is that you and they miss. If you can make them feel discontented they will bring additional pressure to bear on their husbands and friends to support the Escape.

'With this in mind, I am going to make a tour,' Warren continued, standing up and indicating a sequence of farms, villages and Posts which included both Hutton's mountain and Andersonstown. 'One of the most important calls will be Andersonstown. It was there that some of our best Committeemen were lured, trapped or otherwise inveigled into joining the other side, and it is only fitting that we choose the same place to start winning them back again.'

Warren resumed his chair, smiled and went on, 'But this whole area is literally crawling with husband-hungry women, which is another and more selfish reason for me wanting to take you along. The way I see it, arriving in company with a female officer who is well above the average in looks will, as well as showing them that the Committee is no longer composed entirely of misogamists, be the only way of keeping these ravening females at bay and protecting me from a fate which is, the way Sloan tells it, worse than death ... What did you say, Ruth?'

'Sorry, sir,' said Fielding. 'I was muttering to myself about my lack of experience in chaperoning Sector Marshals. And for the other flattering things you said, thank you, sir.'

'Not flattery, Major. Fact.'

'Well, well,' Fielding returned, grinning. 'It seems there

are two good psychologists here . . .'

Hastily, Warren ended the interview before it developed into a mutual admiration society by telling her that he wanted to leave that afternoon and that they both had arrangements to make.

But the preparations for the tour did not go smoothly, and when the hour came when Warren had expected to set off he had what amounted to a mutiny on his hands. It began when Sloan insisted that the Marshal was too valuable a man to risk travelling without a proper escort, and in the same breath, refusing to order his men to a duty which would take them into hag-ridden Andersonstown—nor would he go there himself. It took every scrap of Warren's authority, persuasiveness and invective to finally effect a compromise, which was that a single Committeeman from the Post should act as guide to Warren and an escort made up of six members of Warren's original crew who were fairly proficient with their cross-bows.

The delay meant that they would not be able to stop the night at the farm thirty miles to the south as planned, but the idea of roughing it for the first night out did not seem to bother anyone. They marched in single file with packs on their backs, their cross-bows carried at the regulation Committee angle and with their hair plastered with the strong-smelling grease which was supposed to discourage insects and battlers—if the battlers did not happen to be feeling hungry or mean, and it was only on rare occasions when battlers were not feeling both—and eager to put into practice all the things they had learned as drill at the Post. It was only their guide, an officer named Briggs, who seemed worried. Tactfully but at frequent intervals he suggested that they might not be as proficient as they thought.

But the two-hour trek through the forest, which was often so dense and thorny that Warren longed for Civilian trousers rather than his trim, Committee kilt, did not noticeably damp their enthusiasm and when they reached the road which would eventually lead them to the farm they began to make good time.

It was Warren's first experience of what, until then, had been only a black line on the wall map. The road was little more than an unpaved trail, grass-grown and overhung by trees except where it crossed a river or ravine by way of a strong and surprisingly well-designed bridge. Warren had to remind himself that the road had not been built solely for pedestrian traffic but was meant to take the heavy, metal sections of the dummy and that the whole Escape could fail if just one of those sections was to end up in a ravine.

Three hours before sunset Briggs called a halt, saying that due to their lack of experience it would be better to allow plenty of daylight in which to catch their supper. Then later, when the fires were going well and the men were returning in triumph with the small, rabbit-like creatures which abounded in the forest, Briggs had some gently sarcastic things to say about the large number of arrows which were apparently necessary to kill these ferocious, eight-inch long herbivores. And when there was nothing left of the supper but the appetizing smell he made further attempts to spoil the general air of well-being by talking about some of the horrible accidents which could occur through hammocks not being properly hung. Warren felt a little sorry for him because nothing he said or did could make Fielding and the men stop behaving as if they were all on a glorious picnic.

Some of the things which Briggs had warned them about came back to Warren, however, as he climbed the regulation thirty feet into one of the trees chosen for them to sleep in. Thirty feet was the minimum safe altitude, the height above ground level to which a fully grown battler reared onto its hind legs and with trunks at full extension could not reach. The trouble was that branches at this height tended towards thin-ness, Warren thought as he attached his hammock to the one Briggs had pointed out to him, and checked all the fastenings, and under his considerable mass this one sagged alarmingly. It required a distinct effort of will for him to climb into the hammock even when its fail-safe device—a length of thick rope looped around his waist and tied securely to the branch above—was in position. As he pulled across the flap which was designed to keep out the rain or dew, he was painfully aware of the distance between the ground and himself, and of the fact that he was not going to sleep this night . . .

He awoke suddenly to the sounds of shouting, cursing

and cries of pain. The sky between the leaves above him was light blue and the leaves themselves reflected pink highlights from the rising sun, and in the next tree Briggs was clambering among the branches methodically whacking the undersides of the hammocks with a stick. Warren did not think that the man would subject a Sector Marshal to such treatment, but rather than put it to the test he pulled himself astride his branch and began untying the hammock preparatory to stowing it in his pack. And half an hour later they were on their way, munching on the hard, Post-baked biscuits as they marched.

They reached the Nelson farm just before noon, finding that it comprised a fair-sized log house and a larger but more crudely constructed building for storage purposes, both of them being enclosed by a stockade which sagged badly in two places. A large tree served as the main support and a ladder led up to a platform covered by a skin awning. The platform was above the thirty feet level, a refuge for the Nelsons should a battler succeed in breaching the stockade.

Warren had hoped to stay overnight at the farm and the Nelsons had insisted on him doing so and saying that they could easily accommodate his people between the house and the barn. Despite their offer of hospitality Warren could see that they did not want him there. Mrs Nelson seemed very ill at ease and when he talked to her husband, sounding him on the possibility of his contributing a few hours work a week to the Committee and testing his arguments generally, he found that he was not getting through to the man at all.

The reason, or to be more accurate, the three reasons, were quite obvious. He mentioned them to Fielding as soon as they were alone together.

'Three children,' he said in a strained voice. 'Between six months and seven years. I wasn't prepared for this.'

Fielding was silent for a moment, then she said, 'The Committee keeps records of all arriving prisoners, but they are the only new arrivals which concern them. I did expect something like this, although I would say that three is above the average. You must remember that the dangers of pregnancy are aggravated here—the lack of proper medical facilities and the battler menace to name only two . . .'

'The medical facilities are pretty good, m'am, considering,' Briggs broke in defensively at that point. Warren had not realized that the guide was within earshot. Briggs went on, 'There are some very good ex-medics on the Committee. And among the Civilians, too, of course, but their doctors don't have the same local know-how. Our people, under Hutton, have conducted systematic research into the medical properties of the local flora, and a couple of them have died carrying it out. But these people feel awkward about sending for one of our men at a confinement. They know what we think of bringing kids into a prison world, that such an officer is not likely to take the risk of escaping, or dying, or bringing down Bug reprisals maybe, if he has kids.'

'That,' said Warren with great feeling, 'was what I was thinking.'

'Sorry to butt in like that, sir,' Briggs went on, 'but I wanted to ask permission for our men to repair this stockade . . .'

According to Briggs the farm stockade was in such a state of disrepair that a baby battler could push it over, and as fixing it was a job calling for the concerted efforts of upwards of six men, Nelson was probably waiting until some of his neighbours could come to help with the job. All the indications were that the Committee party would not be staying the night, so Briggs suggested that they do something before they left which would leave a good impression. Besides, if his men fixed the stockade it was the unwritten law that Mrs Nelson would give them dinner and supplies for the journey, and while the farm bread would not remain edible as long as Committee biscuit, for the time it did remain fresh it made the biscuit taste like sawdust.

As he gave the necessary permission Warren thought that words had failed him here and that a nice good deed might salvage something from the situation. He knew that the Nelsons would not mind feeding his hungry mob—Civilian cooking was one of the chief weapons used to convert Committeemen—and he resolved that this good deed should have no other strings attached. He would not even mention the Escape again, and for a while he would be very chary of talking about his ideas to non-Committee people.

53

He was going to have to change his approach, Warren told himself grimly, and develop a whole new set of arguments.

To Fielding he said thoughtfully, 'Mrs Nelson was Senior Warp Engineer on a battleship—she must have more degrees than she knows what to do with—and her husband, a relative moron, commanding a destroyer. It seems a great shame to me that two such brilliant people should be stuck here for the rest of their lives. It's a criminal waste of brains!'

'Yes, sir,' said Fielding.

'Did you see those hand-made books lying around?' Warren went on. 'Full of simple sketches and short words in block capitals. They're *accepting* it, and beginning to think of teaching their children. I think they've given me some useful ideas . . .'

'About founding a dynasty, sir,' said Fielding.

Irritated suddenly, Warren wondered why all psychologists seemed to have one-track minds, the track becoming a deep and well-worn gully where female psychologists were concerned. They had not been that sort of ideas, and he suspected that Fielding knew it as well as he did, but perversely he refrained from telling her about them. Like his arguments, they needed to be worked into better shape. Because it had become very plain to Warren that the main obstacle to the success of the Escape was not, as he had hitherto thought, the Big guardship . . .

Muffled by the thick log walls, but still plainly audible, the Nelson baby began to cry.

CHAPTER EIGHT

If it looked like anything at all, Warren thought, it was an elephant—a large, low-slung elephant with six legs and two trunks which were each more than twenty feet long. Below the point where the two trunks joined the massive head a wide, loose mouth gaped open to display three concentric rows of shark-like teeth, and above the trunks its two tiny eyes were almost hidden by protective ridges of bone and muscle. Between the eyes a flat, triangular horn, razor-edged fore and aft, came to a sharp point, and anything which had been caught by the trunks and was either too large or not quite dead was impaled on the horn while the trunks tore it into pieces or a more manageable size. Because it had no natural enemies and was too big and awkward to profit from camouflage, its hide was a blotchy horror of black and green and livid yellow.

'. . . It is our policy, sir,' Briggs was saying as the beast's heavy tentacles flailed bad-temperedly at the base of their tree, 'to avoid battle with them if at all possible. Only if a party is caught in the open or if they have been retained by some farmer to kill the battler will we fight. So your people don't have to feel ashamed at being treed by a full-grown bull like this one. Killing battlers is a very specialized job . . .'

The rest of what he said was lost as the battler sent its twenty-foot tentacles questing among the lower branches of their tree. It found a thick branch, its tentacles curled around it and tightened, and the tree creaked deafeningly as the battler began lifting its forepart off the ground. But Warren did not have to have the technique of battler-killing explained to him. He had done considerable reading on the subject.

The only quick way to kill one of them was to seriously damage its brain. But this tiny organ was very well protected at every point save one by an inches-thick skull and the tremendous bands of muscle serving the jaw and tentacles. The single vulnerable spot was the roof of the mouth, and a cross-bow bolt or spear driven vertically upwards for a distance of two to three inches brought instant death.

But manoeuvring a battler into a position where this thrust could be delivered was a combined operation calling for great skill, a steady aim and even steadier nerves. It had been found that a superficial wound close to, but not on the eye, caused the battler's tentacles to roll back tightly and its jaw to drop open. This was a purely reflex action lasting for not more than a second, and it was during this period that the hunter had to evade the wildly kicking forelegs and inflict the wound. At the same time precautions had to be taken against accidentally blinding the creature, because if that happened the battler became so maddened that it was no longer possible to kill it quickly and it could devastate the surrounding countryside for days before it finally died. The mouth was the only weak spot and the hunter had to get there first time because he would not get a second chance.

His friends might but not him, ever.

Below Warren the battler transferred its grip to a thinner branch which sagged, splintered and tore free under the strain, sending the creature crashing full length to the ground. The impact was like a minor earthquake shaking the area, then the beast rolled ponderously to its feet and moved away.

'Some of the farmers have succeeded in domesticating them,' Briggs went on as it disappeared between the trees. 'Cows, of course, and they have to catch them very young to remove the horn and tentacles without ill effects. They train them on a diet of grain and killed meat rather than let them catch it on the hoof. You'll see some domesticated cows in Andersonstown. Except for a tendency to kick their wagons to pieces in springtime they're very useful draught animals.

'We can go down now, sir,' he added.

They resumed the trek, following a wide, sweeping curve to the northwest, calling on as many farms as possible until they struck the river, then following it to the sea. There were many farming communities on the banks of the river, comprising anything up to twenty houses sheltering behind a common stockade for mutual protection. His reception in these places was generally less strained than in single farmhouses, the concept of mutual protection apparently stretching to include big bad Sector Marshals, and he was able to meet a great many officers with very useful specialities. He met a large number of their offspring, too, and he was able to test out a number of his ideas and arguments, sometimes successfully.

'I never suspected that you were such a good politician, sir,' Fielding said after one of the visits. 'You kiss babies like you'd been doing it all your life. Or do you *like* the little terrors . . .?'

'Some of them,' Warren had replied guardedly, 'are less terrible than others.'

Since the meeting with the battler his men had ceased treating the whole affair as a picnic, their guide had become much more friendly towards them, and he was even able to indulge in backchat with Fielding and not show any visible signs of strain at this continued verbal contact with a woman. But as they approached Andersonstown, Briggs began to get the look of a man about to face a battler single-handed.

Unlike the Post on the hill overlooking it, no attempt had been made to screen Andersonstown from space observation. It was a small town rather than a village, with well-planned streets of single- or two-storey log buildings, a wooden dock and about thirty boats of various sizes tied up alongside or at anchor in the bay. A semicircular stockade protected its landward side and, because battlers could not swim, the seaward side was open.

Protocol demanded that he first call at the Post.

His intention had been to obtain the names and whereabouts of the most influential officers in the town with a view to visiting them and sounding them out before calling them all together for his major appeal. He had learned by heliograph that Fleet-Commander Peters was also heading for Andersonstown and would arrive in three days time, plainly with the intention of throwing a spanner in the works—respectfully, of course, by calling for a public debate on the whole Escape question. Warren was still too

57

unsure of his position to risk that, so he had to rush through the Andersonstown business and leave before Peters arrived.

But the greater part of the first day was wasted because Fielding insisted that she could not work properly in the uniform issued at their first Post because the outfits worn by Lieutenant Nicholson's girls were so much smarter that she felt everyone was laughing at her.

Nicholson, the Post commander, was a tall, greying but remarkably handsome woman. The uniform which she and the other officers on her all-female Post wore consisted of the usual hide boots, trousers which were tighter fitting than was really necessary and a sort of bolero jacket which laced up the front with leather thongs. Some of the uniforms were laced higher than others, Warren noted, the degree of cleavage apparently controlled by the physiological contours of the officer concerned. Nicholson seemed a bit flustered at having to entertain a Sector Marshal at her Post, but not so much that she didn't crack a smile when she assured him that her girls were all officers and gentlewomen who would respect the privacy of the visitors' quarters, adding that the men in his party might expect to be whistled at from time to time, but that they would be in no serious danger provided they did not whistle back.

It did not take Warren long to realize that there were unsuspected depths to this middle-aged, statuesque female with the nervous and almost impudently respectful manner. She was one of the large number of female officers rejected by the Committee because of the embarrassment of her sex, but that did not stop her from cherishing Committee ideals—like the other girls on the Post she wanted to do everything possible to bring about the Escape.

She was in touch with a great many non-Committee sources of information in Andersonstown, she explained that evening while Fielding and Warren were having dinner with her, and she realized that for the best results the Marshal should put across his ideas and leave before the Fleet Commander arrived to rally the opposition. Lieutenant Nicholson had therefore taken the liberty of arranging a meeting between a representative group of citizens and the Marshal to take place at the Post early next day.

When he heard that Warren felt like kissing the Lieutenant and almost said so. But he checked the impulse. It would have definitely been *lese majeste*, and Fielding would probably have wrung deep, dark psychological meanings out of it.

Warren was surprised to find next morning that the representative group of citizens numbered upwards of two hundred, although he was not surprised to see that the majority of them were girls. Not that he could see them very clearly, of course, because the only direct light coming into the assembly hut was from the trap above Warren's head, so that his table and chair was spotlighted while his audience were mere shadowy rows of faces. But he knew that Nicholson, Fielding and the others of his party were strategically placed among his listeners, the intention being to demonstrate the new and more cordial feelings towards non-Committee officers as well as to answer the sort of questions which could not be asked directly of a Sector Marshal. Warren had deliberately delayed his arrival so that these questions could be answered before he arrived.

He began quietly by outlining the war situation as he, one of the officers responsible for overall strategy, saw it, giving information which was top secret and restricted without the slightest hesitation. It was a picture of a long, costly war which had reached the stalemate of mutual exhaustion. Compared with the large-scale offensive mounted during the early decades of the war, he told them, it would require only a relatively feeble effort now by either side to end it. But neither side was capable of making this effort. The space service demanded a very special type of person, and after sixty years of war the type had become extremely rare.

In a voice which was not so quiet he went on to tell of highly confidential reports which had reached him during and after many operations, of ships which had failed to make rendezvous because key members of the crews had suicided, or mutinied, or shown in some other shameful fashion their inability to withstand the strains of a job which all too often was simply a few hectic minutes of action sandwiched between months of utter monotony. It was a recognized fact that the more highly intelligent and stable personalities could study or otherwise exercise their minds so as not to let them dwell too much on those few minutes during the months before they occurred, or during the equally long post-mortem period when they were returning to base without some of the friends or husbands or wives with whom they had set out. The vast majority of present-day officers lacked these twin qualities of stability with high intelligence and could not withstand this strain, a strain which was being further aggravated by the fact that purely mechanical failures in the ships themselves were also on the increase.

At no time did Warren tell them in so many words that the population of this prison planet, should they return to active service, could bring about the end of the war in their favour within a few years. In every one of them, Warren was convinced, there was a still, small voice saying it for him, and he would only defeat his own purpose if he tried to shout it down . . .

'. . . This place is not escape-proof,' he went on. 'You know enough about the Anderson Plan and the work already done on it to know that the number of officers directly concerned with the capture of the guardship is relatively small. The part which the rest of you will be called to play is also small, but important. From most of you I will require simply your moral support, which *is* important, believe me! From a few others there will be the added inconvenience of moving their families and belongings to safety a few months before E-Day, should the dummy be placed in an inhabited area. As well, I will have to ask for volunteers with the necessary aptitude or interest in the work to help with Major Hutton's research projects, and we will need officers who have the talent for it to donate a few hours a day to compiling text-books and training manuals, or to teaching. Then there is the problem of the children . . .'

Warren could not see faces clearly in that dim room, but he noticed quite a few heads come up sharply, including the bald, shining pate of Anderson himself, and he felt the atmosphere begin to congeal. Just as it had congealed at the Nelson farm and in the other homes and villages where he had brought up this highly ticklish subject.

'. . . As you know,' Warren continued, veering away from it temporarily, 'there are a number of officers here who, although they are extremely valuable people will be unable to return to active service because of age, family ties and so on. Again, some of you have been here so long that your early training may be out of date. That is why I want text-books and training manuals prepared, circulated and studied so that you can be fitted for ship service or, in the cases of older officers or those who have acquired families, for training commands. And while you are busy bringing each other's education up to date, you must give some thought to the children . . .'

Next to the Escape itself, Warren knew, his greatest problem was the large number of children born to the prisoners and the very mixed feelings of these officers regarding them. Coupled with the natural feelings of responsibility and affection towards them there was a definite feeling of shame that they were there in the first place, because no self-respecting officer would even consider having children while on ship service or while a prisoner of war—although it could be argued that the situation here was a case of being marooned rather than imprisoned. But Warren did not seek to chide or criticize, and because they were expecting him to do both they would be relieved when he did neither, and tend to be more sympathetic and less critical of the things he did say. Which was why he stressed the problem of the children and did not even mention the Escape, giving the impression that getting off the planet was simply a matter of time and as certain to occur as the Tuesday of next week.

'. . . Through circumstances beyond their control,' he went on seriously, 'these children have been born into a very primitive world. When they return to civilized society I would not like to think of them being hurt or embarrassed in any way because of illiteracy, or even partial illiteracy.

'And now,' he concluded, resuming his seat, 'are there any questions?'

The first question came within seconds from a man, dimly seen but with a young voice, at the back of the hut. It was a searching, detailed question having to do with certain technical aspects of the Escape itself, proving to Warren that his verbal sleight-of-hand had not worked with one person, at least.

61

'If you don't mind I'll ask Flotilla-Leader Anderson to answer that question,' Warren said, 'After all, it's his plan we're using . . .'

And now I'm using Anderson, too, Warren thought with a growing feeling of shame. The Flotilla Leader could be expected to defend his own plan better than anyone else was capable of doing. But the very act of defending his own brainchild proclaimed that he, the leading citizen of the town which had been named after him, was supporting the Marshal, and if he had not been an old man and grown a little stiff in his thinking he would have realized that he was being used.

All at once Warren felt that he was becoming a quite despicable character. It was not simply the Anderson business which had brought on the feeling, it was the fact that he was lying to everybody, including himself. Without promising anything in so many words he had given the impression that none of the activities which had gone on among the prisoners would be the subject of a court martial, or that officers who had married and had children on the prison planet would not be expected to return to ship service while their youngsters were cared for by institutions. Certainly he would exert every iota of his very considerable authority as a Sector Marshal to bring this about, but he could not be absolutely sure of how the High Command would view the situation here or how the desperate shortage of officers would affect their thinking. And there was his not quite accurate picture of the war situation. It would all have been much simpler if everyone was as keen as the Committeemen, and there had been no children to worry about and no necessity to lie and cheat and play people off against each other.

He became aware that Anderson, who despite his age had retained a firm voice and the habit of command, had demolished the first questioner and that another officer was on her feet. After giving name, rank and qualifications she asked if it was possible for her to volunteer for duty with Major Hutton's research section.

Warren told her that it was.

'But . . . but . . .' she began, then stopped.

'I can see that you are a girl, Lieutenant Collins,' Warren

said, in a tone which was complimentary rather than sarcastic, 'and I have a sneaking suspicion that it is not only patriotic zeal and the urge to escape which is driving you. I am aware of the situation here, you see, and I can say that I have the greatest respect and admiration for officers like yourself who have resisted the pressures to adopt polygamy as a solution. But there are certain aspects of this duty, certain dangers, which you should consider. Not only is the terrain rugged between Hutton's mountain and this town, with the danger of battlers every mile of the way, but at the end of the trip there is the frightful risk of being mauled by two hundred and fifty men who have not seen a girl for . . .'

They laughed longer than the crack warranted, he thought, but when they had settled down again the questions were simply requests for information rather than subtly worded objections. And by the time the meeting ended Warren had eight more volunteers and the questioning had turned to the possibility of obtaining leave on their various home planets after the Escape.

He knew then that he had them, and that there was little if anything that Peters would be able to do about it.

CHAPTER NINE

The complex system of tunnels and chambers had been carved out of the solid rock to duplicate the major corridors and compartments of the great Bug guardship, Hutton told him, and the dimensions and proportions were as accurate as repeated psychological probing of the memories of the prisoners could make them. As he spoke the Major sounded intensely proud of the place—with justification, Warren thought.

'This was part of the mine's original workings,' Hutton

went on, 'since bypassed because of low yield. Someone remembered that the useless tunnel was approximately the same length as the central corridor of the guardship, so we decided to cut out Control, Drive, and shuttle-dock compartments and use it for training assault groups. The later additions and refinements—cross corridors, the Bug living quarters that we know about, dummy controls and Drive housings—were and are useful in training, but they also served as make-work for the people who, with nothing but assault drills to occupy them, would otherwise go stale. Only the more important compartments have been reproduced and the bulkheads are, of course, greater than scale thickness because of the necessity of supporting the system. The entry locks have been made as bulky and difficult to operate as the real ones, but the two things which we cannot hope to reproduce are the Bug lighting and the weightless conditions . . .'

Hutton broke off as another assault group pounded along the corridor past them. The men wore kilts, but there were bulky wickerwork baskets covering their heads and heavy logs strapped to the shoulders to simulate the equipment they would have to carry.

'Those kilts give too much freedom of movement,' Warren said. 'The drills should be made more life-like. Can you reproduce the Bug atmosphere . . .?' He broke off, nearly strangling himself in an effort not to cough.

'It *is* bad today, sir,' said Hutton apologetically. 'The wind must be blowing up the gorge again.'

The base of Hutton's mountain was riddled with interconnecting tunnels, labs, living quarters and the ventilating system which rendered them livable. The air inlets, which also served as observation and communications tunnels, joined the main network at several points while a single outlet used the chimney effect to carry away the smoke and heat from the smelter and machine shops, at the same time drawing fresh air into and through the rest of the system. This outlet emerged some distance up the mountain in a gorge so narrow and steep that the river responsible for its formation fell in a series of spectacular cataracts, the spray from which merged with the smoke so effectively that it was impossible to distinguish them at a distance of a few hundred feet much less from an orbiting guardship. But when the wind blew directly into the gorge, as it did a few times a month, the smoke did not escape completely and the interior of the mountain became barely habitable.

'Is it necessary to duplicate Bug air, sir?' Hutton asked suddenly. 'There are other gases easier to produce which would be unpleasant enough to make them careful without being lethal...'

Warren shook his head. 'These drills have become ... well, drills—something performed without conscious thought. That frame of mind will have to go. Besides, your people working on the assault suits will be that little bit more careful if they know that the wearer can die, during practice as well as the on big day, if they make a slip.'

'The Bug atmosphere is deadly stuff, sir,' Hutton said thoughtfully. 'Getting rid of it afterwards will be a problem. We'll have to evacuate the place and rig fans to——'

'When we've taken the guardship we won't *need* the mountain!' Warren snapped, irritated by the objections. 'Except, that is, as a place to house Bug prisoners, in which case a few tunnels and compartments already filled with their atmosphere would come in handy.'

In the flickering yellow light of the oil lamps Hutton's face, already red from constant proximity to open furnaces, grew even redder.

'I'm sorry, sir,' said Hutton. 'Maybe I haven't fully accepted the fact that *we* will be taking *Bug* prisoners of war again...'

Warren relaxed. 'You will, Major, you will,' he said, smiling. 'And now let's go and give your spacesuit technicians a pep-talk...'

Considering the necessity for concealment and the severely limited resources available, the level of technology inside Hutton's mountain was surprisingly high. As the weeks passed Warren gradually came to know every room and gallery and dimly-lit corner of the place, and his growing familiarity bred admiration rather than contempt. He grew used to the hiss and thump and rumble of the steam engines at every major intersection and the endless belt and pulley systems which transmitted their drive to the mechanical hammers, lathes, air-compressor pumps, and to the fans which augmented the natural ventilation system. He considered normal the anvil chorus from the smithy and machine shops which echoed continuously throughout every tunnel in the mountain, the sound becoming as familiar and distracting as the ticking of a bedroom clock. He became accustomed, when the wind was in the wrong quarter, to conducting staff conferences where every fifth word was a cough, although on those days he tried whenever possible to visit the heavily camouflaged lab out on the mountainside where the gunpowder was produced and where they were currently developing more sophisticated forms of nastiness using wood alcohol, oil and various combinations of organics.

One of the most important things he learned was that Hutton only *appeared* to object to all new ideas and suggestions. The Major had a habit of considering minutely every aspect of a question, the snags first and then the advantages, and Warren's original mistake had occurred because the Major was also in the habit of thinking aloud.

Hutton was now getting all the specialists he needed. From Andersonstown and from farms and villages out to a radius of two weeks travel away they came trickling in. Most of them were girls, of course, but there were enough men among the recruits to tell Warren that he was gaining support for the Escape itself and not merely operating a part-time matrimonial bureau. Naturally the weddings were coming thick and fast and, while there were any number of ex-Captains around to officiate, Fielding suggested that it would be a nice gesture and a considerable boost to a girl's morale to be married by a Sector Marshal.

Warren did not mind. It would serve to improve and strengthen his image, he thought cynically, against the time in the not too distant future when he would have to start getting tough with some of these people.

The time came some eight months after his visit to Andersonstown, on the first occasion that Kelso and Hynds were present at the mountain together. Major Hynds received his orders first.

'You have the communications system and enough non-Committee support to begin our re-education programme,' Warren said. 'I want you to organize the manufacture and

66

distribution of paper and books on the widest possible scale. Every adult on the planet must shortly have enough paper to take initially, say fifty thousand words. Wherever possible there should be consultation between them to avoid duplication of effort, but the main thing is that they commit to paper everything they know. Every fact, theory, background detail or item of personal knowledge regarding their specialties as Computermen, hyperdrive engineers, astrogators, ordnance officers, doctors, psychologists or what have you. Also details of their hobbies and any helpful experiences gained while living on the prison planet. They must organize this data as best they can, bearing in mind the fact that they are preparing the texts from which their fellow officers will study . . .'

Warren broke off, then said sharply, 'I caught the remark about us being lucky that paper grew on trees, Major, but I missed the rest. Speak up!'

'I said, sir,' Hynds answered warily, 'that I suppose I'm the logical one to head this programme, although up to now Intelligence and Education had a very tenuous connection to my mind. But *hobbies*, sir! And planet-side experiences . . . !'

For a time Warren stared silently through the Major. There were very good reasons for preparing books on prison planet know-how, but some of them could not be given to his Staff. He also thought, self-analytically and a trifle philosophically, that while sometimes it was a good thing for a tactician not to let his right hand know what his left was doing—an enemy had two chances of being surprised than instead of one—if carried to extremes the tactician might find that he had surprised even himself. Warren could not understand why, now that everything pertaining to the Escape was going so well, the possibility of its complete failure worried him more and more. Nor could he understand why his disposition towards his Staff and other senior Committeemen continually worsened, even though both individually and as a group, his feelings towards them were little short of paternal. Unless the reason was that he liked and trusted them so completely that he allowed more of his true face to show to them than to less important people, and of the face was that of a mean, short-tempered old man.

Abruptly Warren brought both his mind and his eyes to focus on the Major, realizing as he did so that his blank stare had caused Hynds considerable discomfort. In a tone so warm and friendly, and so different from that which he had been employing of late that it made the Intelligence head even more uneasy, Warren said, 'All hobbies are useful, Major, some more than others. You have two fully operational gliders at Thompson Mountain which you would not have had if certain prisoners had not had the juvenile hobby of building model aeroplanes. And those not directly of use are usually good for morale. So far as recording prison planet experiences for study is concerned, there are two reasons for this.

'First,' Warren continued quietly, 'you must have realized by now that there may be other Bug prisons like this one, and that when we return to service there will be the possibility of us being captured again. I want as many officers as possible capable of forming an Escape Committee wherever they may be imprisoned. The second reason will become plain when you hear my instructions for Lieutenant Kelso . . .'

Not to mention a third reason, Warren added silently to himself as he turned to face the Lieutenant, which he could not go into now or, perhaps, ever.

'I've a big job for you, Kelso,' he went on, 'that of making the people of Andersonstown and the smaller coastal villages into sailors. You will initiate a large-scale boat-building programme—and not just fishing smacks, I want ships capable of carrying passengers, livestock and cargo in useful quantities over long distances. While it is getting under way you will send exploring teams to the other continent and to the islands which link it to us. As well as filling in some of the blank spots on our maps these teams will advise on likely sites for farms and villages which must be built to house the officers evacuated from this continent. As a large proportion of these officers will be townspeople they will have to study the texts produced by earlier farmers . . .'

The expected storm of protest came then, with Kelso as its centre, and Hynds, Fielding and Hutton silent only because the Lieutenant was putting forward their objections much more vehemently than they dared or were capable of doing themselves. And Kelso, Warren noted, was becoming downright disrespectful.

'. . . You can't do it and they won't stand for it anyway!' Kelso was saying. He was beginning to run down and also to drift from the point. 'There's no need to waste men and effort exploring the other continent when there's still enough room on this one, no reason to evacuate anyone to it, and this idea of sending everybody to night school is a sheer waste of time! In your efforts to gain support for the Committee you're undermining it, wrecking it and everything it stands for! Look at all the women coming here, and our location is supposed to be a secret! I tell you the whole damned Committee is fast going civilian and our security is shot to hell . . .!'

'Our security is shot to hell . . . *sir*,' said Warren reprovingly.

Fielding coughed and the two Majors began rubbing their jaws suddenly so that the lower halves of their faces were hidden. Kelso was silent for a long time, his face becoming a deeper red with every second which passed, then he mumbled, 'I—I'm sorry, sir.'

'Very well,' said Warren. Still quietly, he went on, 'Your two main objections are that we don't need the other continent and that we're all going civilian. Well now, I personally do not care, Lieutenant, if the whole Escape Committee goes civilian if in so doing we are enabled to escape. With that out of the way we come to my reason for wanting the other continent, some of which you should not have to have explained to you, Lieutenant—weather observation posts for accurate forecasting immediately prior to the Escape date, and the communications relays to bring the data to us. The Escape itself must be made as foolproof as is humanly possible, which means that no effort or sacrifice however great will be too much if by it we can allay Bug suspicions or otherwise improve the chances of the Escape by the tiniest fraction, and I can tell you that our sacrifices will be considerable. At the same time we will not move until we are as certain of success as it is possible to be.

'Even so,' Warren continued, the rasp coming back into

his voice despite himself, 'it would be criminally negligent and stupidly unrealistic if I did not consider the possibility of failure, or take all possible precautions against Bug reprisals, because we must assume that if the attempt aborted they would retaliate with nuclear weapons. In such an eventuality I would like everyone not immediately concerned with the Escape to be as many hundreds of miles away as possible where, we hope, they will live to try another day.'

The expressions on the faces around him were definitely subdued, Warren thought grimly, and with E-Day just under two years it was not too early to remind them of the consequences of failure. There were still far too many Committeemen who thought of the Escape as something which was always in the future, an event which would never actually come to pass.

Returning his attention to Kelso, he said briskly, 'They will stand for it, Lieutenant, and you will have the job of talking them into leaving. If your well-known charm fails, there are various types of pressure which can be brought to bear. It will be a gradual process, of course, so much so that I doubt if force will be necessary at all.

'Here is what I had in mind . . .'

CHAPTER TEN

The morning of E-Day minus three hundred and eighty was cloudless and hot, with a stiff land-breeze which rendered the heat of the sun pleasant rather than unbearable. Taking advantage of the breeze as well as of the fact that the guardship would not rise for another fifteen hours, one of the new catamarans was racing for the concealed anchorage on the nearest island, ploughing a dazzling white double furrow across the waters of Anderson Bay. The ship passed close enough for Warren to see details of its deck cargo—sections of a glider slipway and a dismantled two-man sailplane—before the bow-wave sent his own boat rocking madly.

Beside him Hutton directed some derogatory remarks after the hurrying cat, then handed Warren a wooden bucket with a glass bottom.

'If you look down there, sir,' he said, 'you'll see the units we've had under two hundred feet of water since last night. I'm going to see if any have sprung a leak.'

At Hutton's signal one of the officers in the larger boat nearby took his place on the overhanging platform which had been built on to its stern, and began carefully hauling in the line which had been attached on the surface to a coloured float. Simultaneously another officer slipped over the side and trod water, his face submerged for minutes at a time as he watched the suit under test rise slowly towards him.

The problem arose because the Bugs had allowed the prisoners to retain their service battledress while divesting them of the associated equipment which converted this shipboard uniform into a short-duration spacesuit. Solving it had turned out to be one of the hardest jobs the Committee had had to tackle.

Various combinations of materials had been tried in the production of home-made substitutes—wood and glass helmets painstakingly carved to fit the metal shoulder rings of the suits, airtanks fashioned from hollowed-out logs and air-hoses of finely stitched leather reinforced along the seams with the foul-smelling glues and sealing compounds which Hutton's researchers had developed. But despite everything the air-hoses ruptured, the log tanks split from internal pressure and the wooden helmets, besides leaking like sieves, retained so much of their wearer's body heat that they were impossible to work in. The answer, so far as comfort and safety was concerned, seemed to be all glass tanks and helmets joined by a short length of cane to which was attached the control taps. But it was not a good answer because the arrangement lacked flexibility and was highly susceptible to accidental damage.

Because the only efficient sealing compound, a tarry substance with a fairly low melting point which set as hard as rock, was nearly as brittle as the glass it sealed, the slightest strain put upon the device by the wearer caused the helmet or tank to crack where they joined the rigid air hose. But it was just not practical to send up an assault group with instructions that, no matter what was happening around them, they were to bend only at the hips . . . !

In the poison-filled tunnels of the guardship mock-up at Hutton's mountain the men had actually carried out a series of drills in such brittle death-traps, so far without any fatal accidents. The men had gone through their manoeuvres grim-faced and stiff-backed and they had insisted that they could do the same under weightless conditions in the guardship, and they had insisted further that no conceivable agency or circumstance, be it Bug, human, or major natural catastrophe, would panic them into making the sort of sudden, unthinking movement which might kill them. Even though there could be no doubt about their bravery, Warren knew some of the hotheads who made up the assault groups and he had done some insisting of his own. To Hutton, that he produce a better answer.

And now the answer was drifting up through the green depths of the bay towards the surface, a grotesque man-shape with a giant, misshapen head and a pouter-pidgeon chest. When it broke surface the officer already in the water detached the weights which had held it to the sea bed and helped lift it aboard. Hutton brought his boat alongside so that Warren could see the details.

To a stiffly-inflated spacesuit had been added a glass helmet and airtanks of conventional Hutton design, the two tanks being mounted in front so that the taps in the hoses were easily accessible to the wearer. The fishbowl, a lumpy sphere of varying thickness whose optical properties left much to be desired, was enclosed at the top, back and sides by an open lattice-work of thin cane shoots which continued over the shoulders and down the back to the level of the hips, and curved outwards to enclose the two spherical chest tanks.

Sealing compound had been used to reinforce the wicker-work shield, a large amount of seaweed had become entangled in it overnight and several varieties of marine life wriggled and flapped in and around it. The object made Warren think of a man who had undergone a rather gruesome sea change, then he had a second look at the spherical chest tanks and decided that it couldn't possibly make anyone think of a man at all.

Hutton said, 'The wickerwork around helmet and tanks protects them against accidental damage, and is open enough to allow unwanted heat to escape by radiation from the helmet. And enclosing the body to hip level in this ... this form-fitting wastebasket means that the arms and legs can be moved freely, even violently, without danger of the air connections coming adrift. It is comparatively light and fairly rigid, sir, and considering the materials, facilities and time available I consider it to be the best workable design to be produced. I'd like your permission to put this one into production, sir.'

The tone of the normally cautious and reticent Major contained the nearest approach to smugness that Warren had ever heard from the research chief, so that it was plain that Hutton thought he had the answer and was expecting a pat on the back for finding it. Warren grunted and scrambled onto the projecting platform of the larger boat, where he lifted the dripping, weed-covered spacesuit carefully and tilted it backwards and forwards several times. He replaced it on the platform and rubbed the green slime from his hands onto the back of his kilt.

'There's at least a pint of water sloshing about in there,' he said, withholding the pat temporarily.

'Sealing the helmet and wicker surround onto an empty suit is tricky, sir. With a man inside to direct the sealing process there should be no leakage.'

Warren nodded, smiling. 'Permission granted. You've done very well, Major. I suppose you'll put Lieutenant Nicholson's girls onto it?'

'Yes, sir,' said Hutton. 'And the girls in town and in the nearer farms will want to help, too. I'd prefer to have female officers exclusively working on this project. They have the temperament for fine work needing lots of patience, and they'll feel that they're making a direct contribution to the Escape, something which they don't feel slicing paperwood or copying text-books all the time.'

73

Hutton paused while a second suit broke the surface and was hauled in, then he went on, 'The wickerwork shield and connections require approximately 110 hours work, although this will come down as the girls gain experience. We'll standardize production into four basic sizes . . .'

As the Major talked on enthusiastically, Warren began to consider the implications of having a workable spacesuit and how it would affect his immediate planning.

The fact that the wickerwork spacesuit project had already leaked to practically everybody did not concern Warren as much as it did people like Kelso and Hynds, who threw up their hands and howled loudly about security. The time was very near when certain matters must be discussed and plans drawn up which *would* have to be kept secret from the general populace, but meanwhile officers talked too much and allowed themselves to be pumped by admiring friends and the process was allowed for, and in some cases actually fostered by Warren. Gossiping was good for morale and news or information gained with difficulty tended to have more weight given to it than that which was given away free.

Warren's eyes were caught suddenly by a motion in the sky which was too regular to be a sea bird. A glider was coming in from the direction of the glass plant farther up the coast, at an altitude which showed that it had made good use of intervening thermals. It banked steeply above the town, sideslipping off surplus height and generally showing off. The underside of one wing bore the white diamond which indicated a trainee pilot.

The glider men were not supposed to talk, but it was general knowledge anyway that they operated in conjunction with the survey catamarans, that the cats which explored the other continent and set up observation posts had, as part of their duties, the construction of camouflaged glider runways on nearby slopes. The job of mapping the other continent had been enormously accelerated by the gliders which, wind and cloud cover permitting, could range anything up to 100 miles inland from their coastal bases. And the cat men were not supposed to talk about the places they'd been—at least, not officially.

So the information leaked out that the other continent

was much superior in every way to their present environment, and the fact that it was a leakage of true information aided Warren's plans considerably. The ground over there was more fertile and at the same time less densely wooded; the mountains, rivers and lakes were higher, longer and more beautiful and the grass was, of course, greener there. But the greatest selling point of all, a stroke of sheer good fortune which Warren could still hardly believe, was that for reasons which were still obscure the native life-form known as the Battler was virtually unknown on the other continent.

So the officers with young families whose farms were in constant danger from these creatures, as well as men who simply wanted a change of scenery, began pressing Warren to evacuate them. The numbers had grown to such proportions that he was building more and more ships to cope with them as well as pulling cats off survey duty. And every time Meteorology forecast suitable winds and a lengthy period of overcast which would hide the operation from the orbiting guardship, a small armada left for the other continent ...

The glider swept out over the bay, banked steeply and headed shorewards again on a course which would take it near a squat, log building set on the edge of the sea which was its hangar. In the boat Hutton had stopped talking and was watching it go over, his expression reflecting the odd mixture of pride, criticism and parental concern of the person who is observing the antics of one of his brain-children.

Because Hutton had had a lot to do with the designing of the latest gliders, it had been he who had insisted that, for ease of operation and subsequent rapid concealment, they should be built to fly off sloping ramps and land on water. He had designed the stepped hull and, when the first three test models had cartwheeled all over the bay because one wing-tip float had dug itself into the water while the other was in the air, he had suggested the sponsons—short, stub wings projecting from the fuselage just above the water line, which removed the landing hazard and in the air added to the lift. It had also been Hutton's idea to use rockets for gain-height when the necessary up-draughts were absent or for extending the glider's range, and he had designed solid-fuel rockets. Hutton was something of an all-round genius, and he was one of the reasons why Warren's plans had gone so smoothly up to now.

Starting today, however, the snags, hitches and deliberate foul-ups would come thick and fast. Peters would see to that.

Warren had not spoken to the Fleet Commander since the day of his arrival. At first he had avoided meeting the other by always keeping on the move. Then gradually it became apparent that Peters no longer sought contact with him, and Warren thought he knew why. Peters probably believed that his arguments for the Civilian viewpoint that first day had, when the Marshal had had a chance to think them over, converted Warren to Peters' way of thinking, and during the past two years Warren had managed to proceed with the Escape plan without disabusing the other of this notion.

Fleet-Commander Peters, Warren had long ago decided was intelligent enough to realize the danger, the long-term danger, of the two factions which had grown up among the prison population. He had not been able to accomplish much against the Committee himself except to pare down their numbers and make them an even tighter and more fanatical group, but he must have hoped that someone with Warren's authority could succeed where he had failed. And one of the ways this could be done, again given the rank which was Warren's was ostensibly to take over leadership of the Committee and wreck it from within.

The steady increase of cordial relations between Committee and non-Committee members, the inter-marrying and the free passage into hitherto secret Committee projects would appear to Peters as a definite galvanizing process. As also would the boat-building programme, the gliders and the opening up of battler-free land on the other continent—not to mention the definite Civilian applications of the re-education programme. True there were good Committee reasons for doing all these things, too, but a tired and ageing Fleet Commander might think that these reasons had been provided by Warren to keep the Committeemen happy while he dispersed them and dissipated their energies in what was obviously Civilian work. And

Warren's recent suggestion of lighting the streets of Andersonstown at night with oil-lamps—a measure aimed at showing the orbiting guardship that they had nothing to hide—could also be taken as a first indication that the prisoners were beginning to accept their lot and settle down.

It had been an elaborate double-bluff aimed at lulling Peters and the opposition which he represented into a false sense of security. But when Hutton's spacesuit went into production the Fleet Commander would not be so old and tired that he would not realize what had been going on, and Peters would react.

With the Fleet Commander alive at last to what was happening, the obvious course would be to hit him as hard and as often and from as many different directions as possible. But Warren had somehow to do these things without losing the respect he had built up among Committee and non-Committee alike. If any particular order seemed too harsh he would have to issue another which took the sting out of it, or at least focussed attention elsewhere . . .

The glider was skimming the surface of the bay, the first step slapping rhythmically along the tops of the waves until water drag abruptly checked its forward speed and it came foaming to a halt. A long, low boat with twelve oarsmen and a towing rope was already shooting towards it to haul it into the cover of its hangar.

It had become almost a reflex these days to cover or otherwise conceal any object likely to arouse the suspicions of the watchers in space. So much so that the action was performed with the same speed and enthusiasm even, as now, when the guardship was below the horizon.

But sight of the glider had given him an idea. It was in connection with one of the points raised by Ruth Fielding at the last Staff meeting about the steadily increasing birth-rate . . .

CHAPTER ELEVEN

Warren said, 'The evacuation must be speeded up, Lieutenant. All personnel not actively engaged on Escape work must be cleared from this area six months before E-Day. You can use the line that I am becoming increasingly concerned over the possibility of Bug reprisals in the event of an unsuccessful attempt. Stress the fact that I'm thinking of *their* safety, and the safety of these children we're continually acquiring who aren't, after all, combatants. You know the drill, lay it on thick. Hynds will give you a list of Peters' supporters and I want you to make a special effort with them. All potential trouble-makers must be moved to the other continent and dispersed before they can organize serious opposition.'

Kelso nodded briskly and bent to make notes. Warren turned to Hutton and said, 'You have a progress report, Major?'

Progress in the Research sub-committee was satisfactory, Major Hutton reported, which from a person as cautious as he was meant that it was going very well indeed. The necessary quantity of assault suits would be ready and tested by the required date, as would the sections of the dummy. Improvements in glass-making had given them a lens which was much more capable of resolving activity around the guardship. Gun-powder, flares and an incendiary material analogous to napalm could be produced in any desired quantity within reason. Hutton concluded by saying that in his opinion no further progress was possible until the position of the Escape site had been fixed.

Warren nodded, then said, 'Hynds.'

'I'm having trouble with the re-education project,' Hynds said. 'The preparation and distribution of material is going fine, but the only texts being studied are those associated with farming. This is understandable considering the numbers of inexperienced people being shipped to the other continent, but I've suggested pretty strongly that more of the time they save in not having to build stockades should be used boning-up on hyperjump theory, nucleonics and such instead of ... of ...'

'Acting like rabbits,' Sloan, from the other side of the table, finished for him.

'Not in those exact words,' Hynds said, smiling but with an uncomfortable glance at Ruth Fielding who was beside him. He went on, 'Apart from this we are up to schedule. The weather posts and communication relays are, or will be, set up and operating in time. Hutton has given us an improved signalling device ...'

The device, Warren knew from his examination of the drawings, consisted of the light from a bright-burning, shielded fire being focussed into a tight beam and directed towards the next leg of the relay. The beam had just enough spread to compensate for the fact that the stations were usually mounted in trees and subject to wind movement, so there was no possibility of it being seen from above. It was used in conjunction with a telescope to increase the range and accuracy, at the same time cutting down on the number of relay stations needed.

'... But the final alignment and full-scale testing of the system, sir,' Hynds concluded, 'must wait until the Escape site has been chosen.'

'Major Sloan,' said Warren.

'We carried out the practice run between Mallon's Peak and a pretended Escape site twenty-three miles away,' the Training chief said in his tight, perpetually angry voice. 'I used eight-man carrying platforms where there were no roads and wagons pulled by domesticated battlers or my men where roads were available ...'

Between the subsidiary smelters at Mallon's Peak and the road two miles away the going had been hard. They used the trees for cover whenever possible, but soon discovered that the more effective the overhead concealment the more difficult it was for the platforms to move. They had the choice of moving like snails undercover or of making rapid progress leaving a trail which a Bug guard would probably be able to spot with his naked eye. The compromise forced on them, crossing open ground on duck-boards laid down ahead of the column and picked up in their wake, involved so much extra work and confusion that Major Fielding's idea for maintaining smoothness and uniformity of effort could not be tried. The men were too busy cursing to have the time, or inclination, to sing.

When the thirty-two platforms with their simulated loads arrived at the road they were transferred into wagons drawn up under the trees which bordered it. Sixteen domesticated battlers, all that could be collected in the area, were already harnessed to their carts and moved off at once, but the other vehicles had to be pulled by his men.

It began to rain heavily.

Under normal conditions—five or six battler-drawn carts and less than fifty pedestrians per week—the Committee roads were adequate. Their top-surface of broken rock cemented together with clay gave good support while allowing rain to drain away quickly. But with sixteen battlers and upwards of three hundred men dragging maximum loads over it in a steadily increasing rainstorm, the surface began to break up. Battlers pulling the leading wagons sank into it up to their knees, which meant that the men harnessed to the following wagons were almost hip deep in the tracks the beasts had made. Then the wheels began to sink into the gradually liquifying surface and the struggling, cursing procession began splitting into three parts.

In the lead were the carts pulled by the domesticated cows, being dragged over or through all obstacles—in one case despite the loss of a rear wheel—by animals whose tremendous strength left them sublimely indifferent to loads, gradients or road conditions. Then came the wagons, bunched together and, falling steadily behind the first group, which were harnessed to officers whose language was not that of gentlemen and who were all too conscious of such factors. And finally there was the group which laboured furiously to heal the deep, muddy scars left in the road so that when the sun came out and dried it off there would be nothing to arouse the suspicions of a possible observer in the guardship.

Three miles from the pretended Escape site the road crossed a bridge which spanned a deep ravine between two thickly-wooded hills. The first part of the convoy was slightly ahead of schedule at this point and the other two considerably behind it, and the bridge had never before been subjected to such a load. But the first three battlers and their wagons went across without the structure showing any visible signs of strain, although the same could not be said for their drovers and handlers, and everyone began to breath easier.

It was when the fourth wagon was at the centre of the bridge, with Sloan sitting beside the driver, that it happened.

A bull battler, old, mean and large even for one of that physically massive species, erupted from the trees near the other end of the bridge. The cow pulling the wagon which had just crossed, reared and plunged sideways as the tremendous head of the bull crashed into its flank just above the middle set of legs. Suddenly it was on its side, rolling off the edge of the road and dragging the wagon with it into the ravine. The driver leapt clear and landed on his hands and knees on the steep slope below the road, scrabbling desperately for a hold on the grass covering it. Before the cow and the wreckage of its wagon hit the bottom of the ravine, and before Sloan could see whether the driver had made it or not, the bull was charging onto the bridge.

The cow harnessed to Sloan's wagon reared and backed away, the lumps below her eyes twisting and throbbing. It was well known that the courtship of male and female battlers was an incredibly violent business—they charged each other and slapped at each other with their twenty-foot trunks, rolling about and parrying each other's blows in such a way that their trunks often appeared to be knotted together. But this was a domesticated battler whose horn and trunks had been excised a few days after birth, and who had never had experience of anything but human beings and other domesticated battlers like herself. So whether the advance of the bull was murderous or simply over-amorous she had no way of defending herself against the heavy tentacles battering at her head and back. There wasn't space enough on the bridge to turn so she reared ponderously and retreated until the wagon, driven backwards and swinging off centre, snagged against the heavy guardrail.

The driver realized what was going to happen before Sloan did and he began sawing frantically at the harness with his knife. Sloan joined him, hacking at the broad straps which hung slack one instant and were pulled tight the next with every movement of the terrified animal. It seemed only a split second after the last strap had parted that the cow's evasive action became too much for the guardrail. With a tearing, splintering sound the battler and a section of rail whisked out of sight, the shock of its impact with the ground shaking the bridge.

Jammed as it was at an angle across the bridge, and so heavily laden that they could not drive over it in time to escape the bull's flailing tentacles, the only possible means of escape was to go under the wagon. Sloan, on the heels of the driver, was scrambling past the front axle when something smashed against the backs of his legs, tightened suddenly around them and began hauling him backwards. He was yanked upside down into the air, one of the bull's tentacles wrapped tightly around his knees while the other one curled around his neck, under one arm and across his chest and together began pulling him in. The gaping red pit of the battler's mouth and the deadly triangle of its horn seemed to rush at him, then slowed an instant before he was impaled as the battler altered its grip.

Both hands were still free. Sloan grabbed the end of the horn and fought to push it away from him.

Had it been a young battler whose horn was still smooth and razor-edged instead of being roughened and blunted by the bodies of too many victims and the passage of too much time, Sloan's terrible grip around the point of the horn would simply have caused him to amputate his own fingers. And if he had not been a man of unusual strength he would have been skewered within seconds anyway. But he held his grip and even tightened it as, forearms rigidly extended and elbows pressed against his pelvic bones for support, the bull started shaking him from side to side.

He couldn't take his eyes off the point of the horn as, pitted with decay and stained with earth, sap and the dried blood of previous victims, it twisted and jerked within a foot of his stomach. His hands were sweating and at any moment he felt they would slip, just as he felt that two steel bands were tightening around his legs and chest as the tentacles coiled tighter and tighter. He couldn't see for sweat and he had no breath to shout for help, although about three hours later, so it seemed to him, help arrived.

The recognized way of killing a battler quickly was a three-man operation aimed at placing a cross-bow bolt through the soft area inside the mouth which was close to the brain, after which the beast died with dramatic suddenness. But such fancy operations were impossible in the cramped space of the bridge, even if Sloan's body had not been in the way, and somebody had thought of using one of the new grenades.

It wobbled into his field of vision, a small, heavy bottle mounted on a throwing stick, burning its last quarter inch of fuse. Sloan did not look at who was holding it because he was suddenly in greater danger from the grenade than he was from the battler. As the grenade was pushed into the bull's mouth he threw every ounce of strength he possessed into an effort to twist to one side.

There was a muffled thump, a surprisingly quiet sound and the battler's mouth jerked open. Blood, brains and fragments of broken glass erupted past him. The tentacles relaxed their hold and the beast rolled on to its side, toppled off the edge of the bridge and joined its last victim at the bottom of the ravine. Sloan would have gone with it if somebody hadn't had a strong grip on his kilt . . .

'. . . But there were no fatal casualties among the men,' the Major concluded. 'One load and two domesticated battlers were lost, but the damage to the bridge was repaired quickly and all traces of the mishap covered. We arrived at the Escape site two hours and twenty minutes late, which time was not completely accounted for by the trouble at the bridge. In my opinion all future practice runs should be made on the route we intend to use on E-Day.'

'Uh, yes . . .' said Warren.

He had never liked Major Sloan as a person and he could not like him now, Warren told himself, but he found himself wishing suddenly that it was possible for one senior POW to promote a subordinate prisoner, or to award a decoration or to do something more meaningful than the bestowing of a few words of praise. He was still trying to frame words suitable to the occasion when Ruth Fielding spoke.

'My non-Committee sources of information tell me that there was another spot of trouble on this practice,' Fielding said angrily. 'Perhaps Major Sloan is too disturbed through reliving his harrowing experience to remember the second incident?'

Sloan and Kelso both glared at her while Hynds and Hutton merely looked uncomfortable, all of which told Warren that they all knew something he did not know and that the reason for him not knowing was because they had deliberately kept it from him. He also knew that it must be important because Fielding was not the sort to tell tales. Warren stared hard into Sloan's ravaged face and snapped, 'Well, Major?'

Sullenly, the other said, 'When we got to the Escape site and officially ended the exercise one of the farmers complained about losing his two battlers and wagons in the ravine.'

Warren nodded. 'I can sympathize with him over the battlers, at least—they have to be caught young and it takes six years of hard, patient work to tame them. What did you say?'

'Nothing,' said Sloan. 'I broke his jaw.'

'You broke . . .' began Warren, and stopped. The sudden reversal of his earlier feelings for the man was so great that he was too angry to speak.

'There was no need to do that,' began Hutton worriedly, but Sloan shouted him down.

'He didn't have to pull his guts out dragging wagons through the mud! He didn't have any trouble at all! All he did was lend us two lousy battlers and then sit back on his fat——'

'I'd have done the same,' Kelso put in hotly. 'I'm getting sick of sweet-talking these civilians into doing things for us, making them think *they* are doing *us* a favour! We do all the real work and take all the risks, and we're supposed to be obliged to *them* . . .!'

'Major Sloan,' Fielding broke in, sarcasm tinging the anger in her voice, 'may be too emotionally disturbed to recall that the man whose jaw he broke was nearly sixty, lightly built rather than fat, and that another non-Commit-teeman who went to his assistance was roughed up by some of the Major's men—although in this case the injuries were not disabling. And that all this strong-arm stuff took place before the two men had any knowledge of the trouble the Major had just gone through...'

'Tempers were short on both sides,' said Hynds quickly, with a warning glance at Kelso. 'A pity, but understandable in the circumstances. But we need the help of these people, Lieutenant, and flattering some of them into giving it—a lot of them give it willingly, remember—is one of the easiest chores facing us...'

'No!' Kelso raged back. 'I'm sick of licking the boots of lousy civilians, deserters! So-called officers who think more of their deserter wives and brats than——'

Warren's fist crashed onto the table-top. In the silence which followed his voice sounded loud even though he was trying to keep it down, and trying to keep the anger and disappointment he felt from showing in it. He said, 'When I allowed a measure of informality during Staff meetings I did *not* give you permission to wrangle among yourselves! I will think about this matter and decide what restitution and disciplinary action is needed. Meanwhile, and if you can refrain from sniping at your brother officers, Major Fielding, I'd like your report.'

But as the psychologist began speaking Warren was giving her only a fraction of his attention. He had seen the smug, unrepentant expressions of the faces of Kelso and Sloan. They knew, and rightly, that he could take no strong action against an officer as important to the success of the Escape as the chief of Training. Hutton, and to a lesser extent Hynds, had registered embarrassment and disapproval at what must look like weakness on his part.

It would have been so much different if they had all been like Hutton, the type of personality which a simple sugges-tion, a hint of a challenge, was enough to call forth maxi-mum effort. And it would have been nice if the whole Escape operation, now that it was going so well, had been free of internal bickering and dissension. Such things in-troduced a sour note into what should have been, what *was*, a bold, imaginative and truly great endeavour. But he had to work with the material at his disposal, Warren told himself, and while Fielding, Hutton and Hynds were easily controlled and directed, Kelso had to be driven with a very light rein. Sloan could not be driven at all. Like a missile with a faulty guidance system, he kept going in the direction he was originally pointed, regardless.

'. . . And to summarize,' said Fielding, winding up her report, 'there are enough non-Committee personnel behind you at the present time to give all the help necessary to the Escape. There is a small but growing opposition to the Escape, but I don't see it hampering us seriously provided we don't furnish it with material . . .' She didn't mention names or even look at Sloan, she didn't have to, '. . . to turn people against us. At the same time the enthusiasm for the Escape which has already been built up can go stale if we don't bring it to a tighter focus. So it would help a great deal in maintaining interest and support if I knew where as well as when the Escape will take place.'

A broken jaw, Warren thought as she sat down angrily, could cause a great deal of pain over a lengthy period of time, especially in a man pushing sixty whose age tended to make healing a slow process. Knowing Ruth he decided that it was the doctor in her rather than the psychologist which was angry, and he felt the sympathetic anger rising again in himself.

Curtly, he said, 'It seems you all need that piece of information and you can't go much farther without it. Very well, I'll give it to you—ten days from now at Hutton's Mountain. There are some jobs I want done first, records and dossiers to be collected—you'll get the details in due course. Meanwhile you can go. All except Majors Fielding and Sloan—I want to see you two.

'Separately,' he added.

CHAPTER TWELVE

Quite apart from her concern over the Sloan incident, Fielding was troubled by the attitude of the original Committee towards those who had joined after Warren's arrival, the men of the assault groups being the worst offenders. Every officer on full-time Escape work wore Committee uniform, but while the uniforms were supposed to be just that, those worn by the first group had certain markings and methods of fastening which set them apart from group two. They were all in this together, she said, but it was as if some officers had graduated from a top military academy while the others had merely come up through the ranks ...

'This is understandable,' Warren broke in at that point, 'when you consider the fact that these men are responsible for the most crucial part of the operation. And I'm afraid, the closer E-Day approaches, the more superior they will feel. I'll do what I can, of course, but it would be better if you stressed the importance of support duties as much as you can so as to make the other party feel more important, too. Frankly, I'm disappointed in the behaviour of some of them myself, but I still think that the men who are going to take the guardship can be forgiven a few misdemeanours.

'At the same time,' he went on seriously, 'I don't want the opposition getting the idea that Committeemen are a pack of hoodlums and bullies, and the Sloan incident could easily give them that impression. That is why I'd like to push through an idea I've had for some time ...'

The idea had had to wait on Hutton's ruling on the feasibility of a glider taking off from water under rocket assist. The ordinary two-man gliders with their considerable payload could be re-designed to rise from the water and stay up when their rockets were jettisoned, but to withstand the stress of such a take-off the wing structure would have to be strengthened, which would increase the all-up weight, the gliding angle and seriously restrict their range. Hutton, however, had come up with a workable compromise.

With a modified hull which would unstick more quickly from the water, a conventional, two-man glider with its entire payload consisting of rocket units could land at its destination *and* take off again provided the passenger was left behind. The passenger, after his work was done, would have to hike to the nearest launching post to await transport home . . .

'. . . The other continent is a glider-pilot's paradise,' Warren continued. 'Mountains, lakes, thermals and updraughts all over the place. The population is very widely scattered and, since that rush of weddings we had last year there is another problem. Being able to send a doctor by glider to the spot where he's most needed, within a matter of hours, will help to alleviate it.

'We'll have to build a lot more gliders,' he concluded, 'but they're useful to have, anyway. And providing fast medical aid when we are so busy with other aspects of the Escape should look good to the non-Committee people, and it should counter the unpleasantness caused by the Sloan incident, don't you think?'

In a strangely neutral voice, Fielding replied, 'It will certainly look good to the expectant mothers, sir.'

Warren stared hard at her for a moment, then he said quietly, 'Believe it or not, I had been considering them, as well.'

She relaxed suddenly and smiled. Warren returned it and went on to give her instructions for picking up some material on Bug psychology he needed and taking it by glider to Hutton's Mountain. He expected to be at the mountain himself by that time and they could work on the material together. When she left he sent for Sloan.

But there wasn't much he could say to the Major apart from commending him for his behaviour during the exercise and deploring his conduct after it. While he talked Warren kept seeing the rain and mud, the wagons bogged down and a bull battler pulling him onto its horn. He fancied he could even see the old, dried bloodstains on it as he fought desperately to push it away, and somehow the commendation took much longer than the reprimand which followed it. When Sloan left Warren shook his head helplessly and tried to clear his mind for more important work.

Andersonstown had grown tremendously over the past two years. The increased boat- and glider-building, the necessity for procuring and storing food and setting up repair facilities, all had added to the size as well as the population of the town. The Escape work went on practically around the clock, which was why Warren had ordered a steady increase in street-lighting at night—at least, that was the reason he had given up to now. But the town, although growing in size, was dwindling in population now as more and more people moved to the other continent. There were scores of storehouses, homes and adjacent farms lying empty, and it was high time they were re-occupied.

Warren spent the rest of the day drafting the orders which would bring mining specialists from Hutton's Mountain to fill the waiting accommodation, the remainder to be filled by a less specialized labour force which would be placed under the direction of the miners. He announced that it was time they did some practice tunnelling in soft ground, and he suggested a spot for it—a thinly-wooded area half a mile inland from the town and a few hundred yards from the road which led northwards to the glass factory. The dirt from the tunnels could be hidden under the trees until after dark when it could be carried away and dumped, or rather spread over, the marshy ground to the south.

The Sloan business still troubled him and he decided that in the circumstances it would be better if he apologized in person, and make restitution in the form of two domesticated battlers from the corral in Andersonstown to replace those which had been killed. The replacements would have to be commandeered again whenever necessary, but he would not stress that point.

An examination of the wall-map showed him that there was a hill-top Post with glider-launching facilities less than ten miles from the farm he intended to visit, and it was almost in line with his final destination at the mountain. A nice long hike would probably do him a world of good, Warren decided, especially since he seemed to be developing a symbiotic relationship with his desk these days . . .

The day of the all-important Staff meeting arrived. Decisions taken today would be irreversible, Warren knew, and subject only to the more minor of modifications. He felt an almost boyish excitement growing in him as he watched his Staff file in and take their seats. Their expressions were tense, puzzled and anticipatory. At the outer entrance they had had to pass two guards with cross-bows at the ready and a brace of grenades stuck in their belts who had requested them to halt and identify themselves— and since the fraternization order had gone into effect two years ago anyone, whether they were Committee or otherwise, had been allowed to go anywhere in the mountain. The walls of the room itself were covered with Bug physiology charts, ambush tunnel layouts and detailed sketches of the dummy and of the guardship interior. Significantly, one of the maps was a chart of the heavens as seen from the prison planet covering the section of space which was thought to contain Sol.

One saw mud ... thought Warren.

Aloud, he said, 'Up to the present, security measures and the classification of information has been unnecessary. Everything leaked, and we liked it that way and even made use of the fact. Henceforth, however, everything which goes on in this room is classified unless I direct otherwise. You will not discuss anything which goes on in this room, even among yourselves, outside it. From now on this room will be locked, sealed and guarded day and night, and nobody except Staff officers will be allowed entrance. The reasons for these measures will shortly become plain, but meanwhile, and before we get down to fixing the Escape site, there is one hard, harsh fact that we all must face.'

He paused, seeing all their eyes on him, then went on, 'It is this. Anything, literally *anything*, which will increase the probability of a successful Escape must be and will be done! I have admitted publicly the possibility of failure, and urged decentralization against possible reprisals, but privately I admit no such thing! We can, we *must*, escape on this attempt! Is this understood?'

They all nodded, some, he noted, more enthusiastically than others.

'Very well,' he continued, 'we'll begin by considering the plan originally put forward by Anderson, the modification it has already undergone at our hands, and the further changes which I intend to introduce now . . .'

Several basic assumptions were called for in the plan, but from what they knew of Bug psychology and military organization these assumptions were justified. The first one was that the location of the prison planet would be unknown to the vast majority of enemy officers on active service. Given that, a hypothetical Bug warship—a small vessel, so badly damaged in battle that its hyperdrive generators kept dropping it into normal space at short and erratic intervals as it limped home—could be brought on the scene. The plight of this hypothetical ship could be such that when it materialized near the prison planet it was forced to land quickly on the night side, its condition so grave that it was unable or unwilling to go into orbit. It would not be aware, naturally, of the other Bug ship already in orbit around the planet, and it could be assumed that after the damage it had sustained in a recent engagement, its crew or even its communications equipment was in no fit state to maintain a round the clock radio watch.

But instead of the unarmed scoutship only containing a pilot, which had been envisaged by Anderson, this one would be the Bug equivalent of a corvette with a crew of four—the assumption, again strongly justified, being that the Bugs looked after their own just like humans and that they would feel more constrained to risk rescuing four of their people than they would one. And it would be a risk from their point of view, because a rigorous examination of data gathered from De-briefing had established the fact that there were only about thirty Bugs on the guardship, that a study of the behaviour of these beings during the transfer of prisoners showed them to be an unusually timid and over-cautious lot, and that it seemed fairly certain that if they weren't actually Bug civilians they were a pretty low order of military.

This was not surprising because the job of guarding a planet called for a phlegmatic disposition and a capacity to resist boredom rather than sharpness of intellect. But while the dullness of mind might play into the hands of the escapers, the proven timidity of the guards represented a real danger. There was always the possibility that the guards, on seeing one of their ships damaged by enemy action and crash-landed, might be panicked into bombing it if, as the original plan called for, there was no sign of life about the wreckage. They might consider it more important to keep the wreck from falling into the hands of the prisoners than take the risk of rescuing colleagues who were probably all dead anyway . . .

'. . . That is why I've decided that the dummy must show some signs of life,' Warren went on briskly. 'Also, the placing of the dummy ship is critical in that it must not be more than seventy miles from either of the two mountains where its metal sections are presently concealed, this being the maximum distance they can be transported while the guardship is below the horizon, and the site must be well served by roads or accessible by sea. No matter how we look at it, this places the site within a ten-mile radius of Andersonstown, and Major Fielding warns me that we may be stretching coincidence a little too much to have the ship apparently land where the farms and prison population are thickest when in the darkness they could have landed anywhere in two whole continents.'

Warren rose and half-turned towards the wall-map behind him, lifting his pointer as he continued, 'Bearing all this in mind I've decided to place the dummy half a mile south of the town. Just here. Major Fielding assures me that this will not arouse Bug suspicions, because what would be more natural than for a badly damaged ship to land as close to the lights of a town as possible, especially on a planet deep inside its own territory where it would have no reason to expect the natives to be unfriendly . . .'

Ignoring Kelso and Hutton, who were fairly stuttering with surprise and incredulity, he went on, 'The advantages of this site are obvious. The non-metal framework of the dummy can be transported to the town and stored long before E-Day, more than half of the metal sections can be moved by sea, which will be much less trouble than by road as well as freeing manpower for the convoy which must come overland, and the accommodation for the people working on the ambush tunnels is readymade, which is the reason for me already ordering Hutton's mining specialists into town. . .'

'But ... but ...' began Kelso, the first of them to become articulate. 'I mean ... that is, I understand now why you insisted on more and more street lighting at night. It seemed stupid at the time ... Uh, sorry, sir, but you know what I mean. But even so, considering the cowardice of the guards, isn't it unlikely that they would risk landing so close to the town ...?'

Warren sat down again and said, 'When the time comes the risk will not seem great to them, Lieutenant. Let's suppose that in coming down so close to town the ship lands practically on top of a farmhouse, setting fire to it with its tail-flare and burning the occupants. This is an unfortunate, but allowable coincidence. Angered by this killing we'll suppose that the human prisoners from town attack this hypothetical ship which, although damaged by battle and a hard landing, still has its C-7 projector operable. The attack will be repelled and in the process all the farms in the immediate vicinity will be burned. I don't foresee there being much left of Andersonstown, either.

'When the guardship rises, which on that day will be an hour before dawn,' Warren continued, 'it will see the fires. Later, when it climbs higher, it will have a bird's-eye view of the nicest little scene of devastation that a Bug could wish to see. Certainly there will be ample evidence that someone is alive and kicking in the dummy ship. The risk of sending down a rescue party will seem negligible, and the Bugs in the guardship should not have their suspicions aroused at all, because the whole area around the dummy will be burning furiously and all our people who are not directly attached to assault groups will be seen to be high-tailing it out of town by road and sea, all making like panic-stricken refugees for all they are worth.'

He stopped speaking to look at the faces around the table.

All Sloan's teeth were showing and his eyes glared their approval. Kelso's face was split by a grin of sheer delight as he murmured 'Man! Oh, *man* ...!' But Warren had been expecting some such reaction from Sloan and Kelso and they hadn't let him down. It was the others who were causing him anxiety now. Fielding had been co-operative, but coldly disapproving since she had learned of his plans.

Hynds was staring at him over his ridiculous spectacles, his mouth grim. Hutton seemed to be still partially in shock, although it was he who spoke first.

'Do we have to destroy the *town*, sir?'

To Warren it seemed odd that an officer whose technical ability and capacity for improvisation had been the greatest single factor in the successful preparation for the Escape should cavil at a little destruction of property. The Major was going soft, and Warren did not know as yet whether to be glad or angry.

'I'm afraid we do, Major,' he said impatiently. 'As I've already told you, *anything* which will in any way improve our chances, goes. And surely you realize that after the Escape the condition of the town will not matter—although here I must stress again that the projected destruction of Andersonstown is information restricted to the present company. Others beside yourself, Major, may have a sentimental attachment for it and may want to make trouble.

'And now,' he went on, 'before we start work on the ambush and communications tunnel layouts, a job which will take some time, there are still some occupied farms near the escape area which will have to be evacuated. The people in them are being stubborn and I'd like to discuss methods of getting them out—short of stampeding a herd of battlers through their stockade, that is . . .'

Kelso and Sloan laughed, Warren noted, but not the others.

CHAPTER THIRTEEN

From the observation platform in the highest tree in Nicholson's post the town looked peaceful and innocent, which was exactly how it was supposed to look since the guardship was overhead at that moment. A few fishing catamarans drifted aimlessly on the bay and in the streets the people were deliberately moving slower than usual, giving the impression of people who did not have much to do. Warren nodded approval and swung his telescope to bear on the Escape site half a mile to the south. It was the afternoon of E-Day minus one hundred and seventy two.

Beside him Hutton said 'The ambush tunnels and ready rooms are complete, sir. Half an hour's work will break them through to the surface once the dummy is in place. We start on the communications tunnels now, one to the observation and attack point in that clump of trees and another to link up with the hollow to the right. I thought of linking all attack points with secondary tunnels in case the shuttle lands in the wrong spot and causes a cave-in. If I can keep work parties on it round the clock we can finish in time.'

'Do that,' said Warren.

He was thinking that now he would have to send for Major Sloan's commandos, that Hutton's suit and explosives technicians would also have to be brought in and billeted in Andersonstown, and that the place was going to become devilishly crowded if he couldn't talk the remaining non-Committee people into moving out. As well, with the influx of men and material it was going to be impossible to maintain the pretence that all the tunnelling that was being done was simple practice. And when the non-Committee people realized that the actual Escape site was to be within half a mile of the town, they would react. Some of the smarter ones would take a closer look at the tunnel layout, and at the type and quantity of material currently being moved into the town, and they would be able to piece together his plan in its entirety.

But the assault groups would have to accustom themselves to moving in bulky spacesuits through narrow, dimly-lit and often muddy tunnels, and to waiting for hours on end in those conditions. They would have to learn to operate effectively after long periods without food or water, and cope with the problems which must crop up. Warren had no other choice.

'Simulating the projector damage worried me, sir,' Hutton said, bringing Warren's mind back to the here and now.

'To achieve the effect you want will require enough powder and fire-paste to start a non-nuclear war, and making such a quantity means hurrying the manufacturing process, which will add tremendously to the risk of accidents. Storing it in town is asking for trouble, too, considering the way some of the tunnellers act when they come off duty. One wrong move and the town would go up, prematurely. That would certainly tell the Bugs we were up to something . . .!'

Compared with some of the difficulties Hutton had overcome these were as nothing. The answer was simply to tighten up on safety precautions, but Hutton was acting as if the whole Plan was in jeopardy. The Major, Warren thought angrily, was beginning to drag his feet.

A lot of officers these days seemed to be dragging their feet or were visibly having second thoughts about a great many things, and the odd thing about it was that most of them were Committeemen of long standing, not recruits. With less than six months to go, enthusiasm for the Escape should have nearly reached its height . . .

On E-Day minus one forty-three Fleet-Commander Peters arrived at the post, unescorted and requesting a meeting. Warren granted the request and Peters was shown into his office, a room not nearly so sound-proof as the Staff room in Hutton's Mountain, but then Warren had the feeling that many of the secrets he had been trying to keep were secrets no longer, otherwise the Fleet Commander would not have been there in the first place.

He stood up when Peters entered, a courtesy he had not extended to a junior officer for more years than he could remember, but when the Commander took the chair on the other side of the table without either saluting or saying 'Sir' Warren sat down again, violently.

'I don't mean to be disrespectful,' Peters said, obviously reading Warren's expression and feeling that some sort of apology was called for. But the bitterness in his voice robbed it of all warmth or sincerity as he went on, 'It is simply that I can't bring myself to salute while wearing this caveman get-up—I'm improperly dressed—and I have no right to do so in any case since I passed the compulsory age of retirement four months ago. I'm afraid I really have become a civilian, Marshal.'

Hutton and Hynds and a few others had begun to whine at him. Warren thought angrily, and now the chief member of the opposition was doing it, and the self-pitying whine of the aged from an officer of this man's stature sounded worst of all. It took a great effort for Warren to alter his expression and say pleasantly, 'We'll have to escape now, Commander. Four months back pension plus retirement bonus is too much to give up . . .'

'You don't have to humour me, Marshal,' Peters said quietly, 'I'm not as old as all that.'

Warren stopped trying to be pleasant. He said, 'You wanted an interview. You've got it, but you'll have to make it short.'

Peters bowed his head, muttering something about no longer being entitled to the courtesy due his rank and that he was foolish to expect it, then he looked up and said, 'I seem to have started this all wrong. I'm sorry. What I came for was to ask you to cancel the escape attempt, permanently . . .

'Don't laugh at me, dammit!' he raged suddenly, then in a voice filled with quiet desperation he went on, 'You can do it if you want to. I know that. In two and a half years you've done things which I thought were impossible! Making Kelso run errands for you and like it, when we were all expecting the exact opposite. Making hidebound Committeemen fraternize, and very often marry, non-Committee officers and generally turning the Committee upside down and inside out—and making them all like it! Not to mention having all the married officers with children practically eating out of your hand because you expressed concern for their safety and lack of proper education. All this, with the build-up of non-metal technology, communications, exploration and now even an efficient medical service, was simply an elaborate ruse to disarm our suspicions and to clear the escape area of everyone but your personal bully-boys!

'And don't try to deny that Andersonstown will be the escape site,' Peters went on angrily, 'Because too much work has gone into the so-called practice tunnels. There are other indications, too. You probably intend to destroy the town!'

Warren did not try to deny it.

'When you deliberately avoided meeting me,' Peters continued, 'and when you kept doing all these unorthodox things I thought you were on our side and were boring from within, or should I say leading the Committee to its own destruction. There were times in the early days when I could have hamstrung some of your projects, but I helped them instead—quietly, of course, so as not to make Kelso and the others suspicious. I know now that I was deluding myself, but I thought that a person with your ability and authority would also have the intelligence to see that . . .'

He broke off, shaking his head. Pleadingly, he said, 'I'm making a mess of this again. I'm sorry. What I want to say is that there is still time to make the bluff the actuality and the Escape the ruse. You can do it. I have never in my life met anyone else capable of doing it, but you could. Please.'

Warren was silent for perhaps a minute, staring into the other's desperate, pleading, embittered features, and feeling impatient and sympathetic and not a little embarrassed by compliments of such blatant crudity. Then suddenly he shook his head.

'I won't cancel the Escape just because you ask me to,' he said. 'Even if you gave good reasons, which you haven't up to now, I wouldn't do it. You are aware of the situation as it was when I arrived here. If I hadn't got tough there would have been a civil war on the first day! And I give you credit for intelligence somewhat above the average, Commander, so that you must realize where that situation must lead. The outbreak of fighting between Escape Committee and Civilians, stabilizing itself with the farmers and other civilians submitting to the authority of local Committee posts which would furnish protection against battlers and the raids of neighbouring Committeemen would shortly have become indistinguishable from slavery, and then more violence as the Posts recruited and trained their slaves to fight for them and expand their respective territories. You must realize that a descent into savagery would be swift and all too sure, and that succeeding generations would grow up in a feudal culture which would get a hell of a lot worse before it got any better. I'm thinking in terms of hundreds of years . . .!'

Warren broke off, realizing that he was almost shouting, then went on more quietly, 'One reason for the Escape is that I can't allow such a criminal waste of high intelligence and ability to occur. Another is that the training and ability of these officers could very well win the war for us if they were returned to active service. Yet another, and perhaps the least important of the reasons, is that it is the duty of any officer when taken prisoner in time of war, no matter what the circumstances, to make every effort to escape and rejoin his unit . . .' Warren's tone, still quiet, took on a cutting edge. '. . . Do you still believe in a sense of duty, Commander?'

Peters shook his head violently, but it was probably in anger rather in simple negation. He said harshly, 'Those are good reasons but they are not good enough to excuse what you're going to do. Surely you see that yourself—unless initiating and pushing through large-scale operations regardless of mental or physical suffering is an occupational disease with Sector Marshal, and I don't want to think that of *you*! As for duty, traditions of the service, patriotism is a matter of inner conviction, while those of lesser intelligence, such as the type of officer the service is producing now, have to have it conditioned into them!

'Surely you can see that it is the older and more highly-trained officers who tend to go civilian,' Peters rushed on, 'and that the later arrivals make the most fanatical Committeemen. You can't avoid the implications of that. It's my guess that even now, within the Committee and possibly even among your own Staff, things have begun to go sour on you—people having second thoughts, wondering if they are in fact doing the right thing. Because it is the sensitive, intelligent people who are the stuff of traitors. And you could help subvert them. Even now you could turn enough of them against the Escape to——'

'That's *enough*!' Warren thundered, his anger at this man who had awakened all the self-doubt and mental turmoil which had made sleep nearly impossible for him in the early months of captivity, and which he had thought were settled at last, was so overwhelming that for several seconds he could not speak. But finally he said, 'We *must* escape, Commander. I've given this a lot of thought, believe me. Escape is the only real solution and I can conceive of no possible argument which will change my decision——'

'You mean you want to go on playing with your soldiers!' Peters broke in, his face and even his balding scalp blotchy with anger. 'Earth, the war and the glorious traditions of the service are just excuses to let you go on feeling important! To let you make a last, heroic, stupid gesture which nobody but your fellow prisoners will ever know about . . .!'

'Get out, Commander!' said Warren thickly.

'Very well!' said Peters, jumping to his feet. 'I'm wasting my time here anyway, trying to talk sense to a stupid, narrow-minded martinet with delusions of grandeur! But I'm warning you, Marshal, I'll do everything possible to stop this escape short of killing you . . .!'

'I'm sorry *Mister* Peters,' Warren said coldly, as he also stood up. 'Sorry that you had to add that qualifier. It put me under an obligation to stop short—not too far short, perhaps—of killing you if you try to hamper me . . .!'

It was some time before Warren's anger subsided to the point where he could feel regret at his mishandling of the interview. He should not have been angered by the other's initial lack of courtesy or lost his head when Peters had got home with the jab about his best officers being potential traitors. He should have kept his temper and remembered that the Fleet Commander was an old, embittered man whose mental processes had hardened too much for him to see that there could be no easy way out of Warren's dilemma . . .

Abruptly, Warren strode out of the room and the Post, his intention being to inspect the new tunnels, chat with the officers working on them and generally to occupy his mind with any constructive activity which presented itself. For the thought had come to him that it might not be only the Fleet Commander's mental processes which were hardening, and with that thought came rushing back all his other doubts.

CHAPTER FOURTEEN

At first Warren thought that one of the domesticated battlers had broken loose and was wandering the streets, grunting and scuffling at the ground with itching stub tentacles. But when he turned the corner he saw that it was a fight.

The light from the nearest street-lamp was too dim to show subtle variations of uniform, but it was obvious from the silent ferocity of the battle that the men themselves were in no doubt as to who was who. There were seven of them, four against three, and they were tearing into each other with hands, feet, heads and in one case teeth. Individually, they were equally matched in size and weight, but the three appeared a little faster, more vicious and fractionally less drunk than the four. Warren started forward to intervene, but before he had taken two paces it was all over. The victorious three moved away, one of them limping slightly, towards the noisy, brightly-lit storehouse which had been converted into an assault group club. The defeated four were on the ground, one on his hands and knees with what, in the bad light, looked like fresh black paint covering his face, another was clutching his stomach and being sick and the other two weren't moving.

A watchman came trotting up, stopped and began blowing the call for stretcher-bearers, a signal which had become all too familiar of late. He kept on blowing, the whistle clenched so tightly in his teeth that Warren thought he would bite through the wood, until there was a distant acknowledgement. He knelt beside one of the motionless figures until the stretcher-party arrived, then rose, cursed horribly and trotted back to his post.

As he joined the group around the injured men, Warren made a mental note to speak to Hutton about some of those watchmen. Their job was to guard the explosives stores against the wanderings of unauthorized or irresponsible— or more simply drunk—personnel and there their job ended. But recently they had been taking on some of the more general duties of policemen. They didn't seem to realize that horning in on what was essentially a private fight was a sure way of getting hurt, as well as arousing the dislike of both parties.

Warren was not surprised to see that the stretcher-party were all girls. With the spacesuit building programme nearing completion and the book-making and copying projects moved to the other continent there was little else they could do except staff the hospital which had been set up to treat injuries among the tunnellers. They were temperamentally suited to the job, of course, and while Warren had been irritated when they had refused to be evacuated with the rest of Nicholson's girls, he was now glad that they had stayed. The doctor in charge of the party was a man, however.

He gave his lamp to Warren and told him exactly where to hold it while he examined the injured men. Considering the fact that their heads were often less than six inches apart there was ample light to see each other's faces, but the doctor pretended not to recognize Warren—acting on the assumption, probably, that he could say things to a chance helper which he most definitely could not say to the Marshal.

'. . . Three ribs gone and maybe a ruptured spleen,' he said as his fingers explored the injured man's chest and abdomen. His voice was singularly lacking in the quality known as professional calm. 'Those injuries he got while lying here on the ground, *after* he was out! I suppose it's one way to get a non-Committeeman to leave the area . . . And look at his face, and at that ear? Damn near bitten through! Animals fight like this . . . *Animals* . . .!'

Warren listened silently while the other relieved his feelings at some length. When he finally got the chance to speak his voice was grim and at the same time pleading. It was a tone he had had to use so often of late that it had begun to sound insincere even to himself.

'I don't like it any better than you do, Doctor,' he said. 'It grieves me to see officers who are supposed to be fighting the common enemy fighting among themselves instead. But with just five weeks to go everybody is getting tensed up. It's natural—the situation rather than the people are to blame. And the riotous night-life we go in for . . .' He laughed briefly, '. . . which nobody expected or prepared for. But the first prisoners learned how to make beer, and stronger stuff, from the local vegetation, and officers who have been digging all day or night in hot, badly-ventilated tunnels or training in practice suits without food or water for twelve hours have a right to a little relaxation. Our trouble is that we can't standardize the strength of the brew, and when people get drunk they are sore inclined to fight.

'Since the tunnel sabotage it has been much worse, of course . . .'

On E-Day minus fifty, in an attempt to control the growing disaffection between the assault groups and the labour and supply force, Warren had ordered a special inspection. The inspection was doubly special in that it was to be the first time in more than two years that all work on the Escape ceased in Andersonstown and the surrounding district, and that while it was taking place every man and woman wore their green shipboard uniform instead of the permutation of kilt, harness or shapeless leather garments normally worn. He had ordered this so as to point up the fact that there was no basic difference between them, that they were all brother officers . . .

The sour note became apparent as soon as Warren mounted the review stand to address them. Simply it was that the uniforms were not uniform. Stupidly he had forgotten that the Committeemen treated their ship's battledress as their most treasured possession while the others had worn theirs until it was in tatters before being forced to change to the home-made clothing. So that even when they were all dressed the same it was still glaringly obvious who had been Committee and who had not. Despite this Warren had not done too badly.

He had begun in much the same fashion as he had opened previous speeches and arguments, by contrasting living conditions here with those of civilization, and he had moved on gradually to reminding them of their obligations to themselves and to the human race. He told them that if they were to passively accept their imprisonment it would be the first step in a regression towards eventual savagery and such a shameful, such a calamitous waste of intellect and training did not bear thinking about. To escape was their simple duty, therefore, and not something which could be argued about.

But the Escape would demand great sacrifices from all of them, and in many cases the suffering would be psychological as well as physical. They would have to blunt their finer sensibilities, forget that they had ever been nice people, and remember only that they were going to bust out of this planet-wide prison no matter what.

Warren did not know at what stage he had stopped consciously using verbal push-button, at what point the fierce pride he felt in these splendid officers drawn up before him and the truly glorious undertaking on which they were engaged began to overcome him. Some of their duties appeared more important than others, he had told them, but they should remember that the work of the battler drover, the assault commando and the lonely officer at a relay post a thousand miles away was equally necessary to success. After the Escape, history would accord them equal honour and homage as the heroic officers who had never given up, who had achieved the impossible and who would be chiefly responsible for restoring peace to the Galaxy. He wasn't sure at what point it was that he knocked over the speaking trumpet Hutton had rigged for him, but by that time he was shouting too loudly for it to matter. He had lost much of his control, and the pride he felt in them and in what they were doing communicated itself to the officers ranked before him. Suddenly they had begun to cheer, the officers in tattered uniforms as loudly as the others, and Warren had dismissed them shortly afterwards because there had been a distant danger that he would have grown maudlin about them if he had gone on.

It had been during these proceedings that the pumps used to clear the main ambush tunnel of seepage had been dogged open, and the ford across a nearby stream converted into a low dam with stones and mud. The water level had risen only a few feet, but this had been enough to send water pouring back along the wooden pipe which normally emptied into the stream to flood the tunnel.

A full week was needed to repair the damage, which

necessitated evacuating the whole tunnel system while the water was pumped out and the tunnel roof and walls, so softened by the action of the water that they were in imminent danger of caving in, were baked hard with charges of fire-paste. Assault men had to place and fire these charges, and while they were burning, the atmosphere inside the tunnels was unbreathable. It was a severe test for the space-suits and for the tempers of the men wearing them. The suits had tested out fine, but the tempers, judging by the condition of the four men at present on the way to the hospital, had not.

It had angered Warren that the assault men no longer trusted the labour and supply force, even though the majority of the latter were undoubtedly loyal to the Committee. Sloan's commandos had begun to mount an unofficial guard at certain vital points, which angered the hard-working tunnellers and explosives technicians even more. The constant bickering and snarling and, at times, outright bloody violence which had followed his 'We're all brother officers' speech had not improved Warren's own disposition. He seemed to be constantly angry these days, but the anger, he had found, was a good cure for his self-doubts.

Not all the fights were as vicious as the one he had just witnessed, however. Perhaps, he thought cynically, the fighters had not been entirely able to forget that they were nice people. And frequently he came on officers singing as they marched off shift or on the way to training areas, usually to a blood-curdling accompaniment of signal drums and wooden whistles. Tunes like 'Waltzing Matilda' and 'John Brown's Body' and 'Colonel Bogey'—the latter a song which, according to Hynds, had never possessed a printable lyric in the three-hundred odd years since it was written. Not all the songs were martial, however, a fact which bothered Kelso and Sloan so much that they brought it up at the Staff meeting on E minus thirty-six . . .

'. . . Stupid, sentimental songs like that are bad for morale!' Kelso had said. 'Hutton's people are the worst offenders, singing about peace and Christmas and . . . and . . . Some of the words are *anti*-war—pacifist stuff, and downright subversive! "Where have all the flowers gone?" indeed! Suppose the commando unit get infected with this sort of tripe . . . !'

'Anything which makes them want home,' Warren had told him sharply, 'is all to the good.'

Warren had wondered briefly how it was possible to both like and dislike what he was doing, and the people who were helping him do it, intensely at one and the same time.

In Hutton's Mountain, strangely deserted now that the metalwork was complete and most of the technicians were in Andersonstown making explosives, he came on men adding the finishing touches to the dummy sections—lavishing the patience and care of a Michaelangelo on the job of making their sections of plating showing the pitting indicative of a too-fast entry into atmosphere, the buckling and discolouration of a near-miss by a beam weapon and the deep, bright scratches caused by it running through the exploding fragments of sister or enemy ships. But the real artists he saw were in Mallon's Peak where a smaller and more specialized group were preparing the airlock section of the dummy.

During a brief trip to the other continent with Hynds he saw a glider medic misjudge a landing. It had been dusk on a still evening with the surface of the lake as smooth as glass, and it had looked as if he had calculated his touchdown about twenty feet below the actual level of the water. They had reached the floating wreckage in time to extricate him before he drowned, but the whip action of the crash had broken his neck and he had died shortly afterwards. In the carefully neutral voice which he always used these days when Warren was around, Hynds had remarked that the planetary population figure would show no change, as the confinement which the medic had been called to had proceeded normally and a girl baby had replaced the man who had checked out.

During his restless and often unescorted wanderings he came on groups of men lying sprawled out in the long, hot grass, on their sides or propped up on their elbows as they watched their instructor developing some aspect of the attack with the aid of diagrams tacked to a tree-trunk, and occasionally asking highly pertinent questions in deceptively casual tones. Or men suspended from high branches by a single rope around their belts, swinging and twisting and sweating inside wickerwork shields while they shot their cross-bows at ridiculously small targets. In weightless conditions, spin would be set up by the reaction of any projectile-firing weapon, and this drill was to accustom the men to hitting targets which whirled and twisted around them. Their instructor would yell advice about shooting from waist level to minimize spin, and often the men would miss their targets completely because they were incapacitated by laughter as much as dizziness.

Some of the men, the assault groups in particular, seemed to get a kick out of Warren's informal, unexpected visits, especially when he joined in their drills. With others his activities simply made them uncomfortable. But for many weeks he had felt an increasing need to reassure himself that his plan was going well, that he was doing the right thing and that the Committeemen would still follow him. Like some latter-day Haroun al Raschid he wandered his kingdom in an attempt to discover what his people were really thinking. When he found that often they did not think the way he wanted them to, Warren lost his temper to such an extent that his show of democratic good-fellowship must at times have seemed like sheerest hypocrisy.

But everyone laughed or lost their temper or lashed out too easily these days. E-Day was rushing down on them now, and tension had become a major constituent of the air they breathed. By Minus Twenty-three the domesticated battlers had been dispersed to the neighbourhood of the two mountain workshops, where singly or in small groups they would practice with dummy loads along the routes they would use on E-Day. The gradual build-up of shipping in the bay, no longer concealed so as to suggest to the guard-ship that the POWs were settling down to a programme of exploration and expansion, was sufficient to evacuate essential records and personnel. The long-range communication system had been tested and the weather forecasters were guardedly optimistic.

Warren's own feelings closely resembled those of his meteorologists, until on E-minus Twenty-one a glider coming in to land on the bay discovered the second major act of sabotage.

CHAPTER FIFTEEN

'It's one of the trees giving cover to Number Two Attack Point,' said Major Hynds worriedly. 'Cutting it down when there is no reason to do so will look suspicious to the Bugs, and leaving it as it is won't be any better because it will stand out like a beacon. The tree is dead, of course—the bark was stripped from around the trunk close to ground level, the damage being hidden by the underbrush until the glider pilot noticed the colour change in the foliage and called our attention to it.

'I don't know what we can do about it, sir,' he ended grimly. 'In three or four months the leaves will drop off, but before that, within two weeks from now, the leaves will have turned bright yellow.'

'Yellow,' said Kelso viciously, 'How very appropriate! I've always said Civilians were no good. They're nothing but cowards and lousy deserters, and we should have kept a closer watch on them——'

'We need those lousy Civilians, Lieutenant,' Hutton broke in quietly. 'And you can't put a guard on every tree.'

For an instant Kelso looked as though he wanted to hit the Major, and Sloan's expression indicated that he might join the Lieutenant in making a combined operation of it. Fielding and Hynds looked worried, but whether over the danger to Hutton or the threat to the success of the Escape was open to doubt.

Hutton himself seemed to be the most unconcerned officer in the room. Warren was beginning to have suspicions about Hutton.

Normally a big, mild, almost shy individual, he had recently taken to baiting Kelso and Sloan during Staff meetings—although always quietly and politely. Warren could not help remembering Peters' remarks to the effect that the higher an officer's intelligence the more likelihood of his becoming a traitor . . .

'All right,' said Kelso, visibly controlling himself. 'There are a lot of things we *can't* do, like putting our heads between our knees and spitting until we reach escape velocity. But if I could make a constructive suggestion, sir, how about stripping the tree of its greenery, then bend its branches into those of the adjoining trees, securing them with ropes and working the living foliage in and around the stripped branches. It would have to be done carefully, of course, and inspected from the air by glider to be sure it looked right . . .'

'Impossible, I'm afraid,' said Hutton again. 'It would be good enough to fool the guardship, Lieutenant, but you forget that when the dummy is in place they'll probably soft-land a probe in the Escape area. What would fool a telescope will not pass what would amount to a microscopic examination. If the Bugs see a stripped tree with branches from adjoining trees tied across it . . . Well, they'll be as jumpy and suspicious as it is possible for Bugs to get in any case, and such a blatantly artificial camouflage is taking too big a risk. It would be better to leave the tree as it is.'

'That is your suggestion, Major?' asked Kelso, his tone carrying more sarcasm than befitted that of a junior officer. 'Leave the tree as it is?'

'Yes,' said Hutton. He looked at the faces around him, then almost apologetically he went on, 'Of course I'd also suggest getting off a signal to all Posts to have their men go out and kill trees, the same type of tree, in the way in which this one was killed. The idea would be to suggest that some kind of infection is attacking this species of tree, and with trees turning yellow all over the continent I don't think the Bugs would notice that ours had turned yellow a little earlier than the others . . .'

It was the answer, of course. Warren's earlier suspicion of Hutton began to fade, although he still thought it a pity that the Major could not have given his answer without sniping at Kelso.

'Nice thinking, Hutton,' he said warmly. 'I don't mind admitting that I was badly worried there for a while. Now is there anything else needing attention before the signals go out . . .?'

Major Hynds shook his head, automatically catching his

spectacles as they fell off. Sloan and Kelso were glaring at Hutton, who stared politely back at them. It was Ruth Fielding who spoke.

'Two days ago,' she said, using her clinical voice, 'there was a bad accident with a battler at the Telford farm. Three men were badly injured, two of whom were dead by the time they managed to get them to the hospital. The third man, Flotilla-Leader Anderson, died this morning. He talked to me before he died, and if the Lieutenant doesn't mind I'd like to know what exactly happened at that farm.'

Kelso and Sloan switched their angry gaze from Hutton to Fielding, but when the Lieutenant turned to face Warren again there was anxiety as well as anger in his expression.

'I've had that farm under observation for three months,' Kelso said carefully, 'and during that time nothing resembling farming has gone on there. The place has been occupied by as many as seven officers at a time, all members of the opposition. Fleet-Commander Peters has stayed there many times recently, and I'm morally certain that the tunnel flooding operation was mounted from there. That's why, when I was with the battler-hunting party in that area I thought of mounting a small, unofficial operation on my own . . .'

Having flushed a battler within half a mile of the farm, Kelso had hit on the idea of wounding it instead of killing it outright with one of the new grenades and herding it towards the Telford stockade. This was a very chancy business, necessitating members of the party running just a few feet beyond reach of the beasts tentacles to make sure it followed them, but they managed it without anyone tripping and being trampled to death. When the battler had been within fifty yards of the stockade and properly lined up they had blinded it and run clear.

Telford had been asked to move countless times, his farm being one of those due to be burned on E-Day, but he had refused point-blank to move to the other continent or to give a reason for staying put—being a ringleader of the saboteurs was not a reason which could be mentioned aloud to Committeemen. The idea therefore had been to run a battler into his stockade to make him realize that his farm was no longer a safe place, to give him the idea that he was no longer wanted in the area. It had been meant purely as a warning, with absolutely no harm intended. But the battler had been unusually large and Telford's stockade had been in a serious state of disrepair. Instead of shaking the stockade and scaring the occupants of the farmhouse the battler had gone right through it. By the time Kelso and his party got to it with grenades it had gone through the farmhouse, too . . .

'. . . We dug them out of the wreckage and got them to hospital as fast as we could, sir,' Kelso went on soberly, 'but the only one we thought might make it was Flotilla-Leader Anderson. I . . . I'm very sorry about this, sir. I only meant to frighten them off. W-we were looking on the whole thing as a joke, sir. I wouldn't . . . I mean, it's Anderson's plan we're using, even if he did go civilian at the end . . .'

You have to look at both sides, Warren thought desperately, striving to hold back his anger. He had to look at the picture of his Committeemen laughing as they played tag with the most deadly menace on the whole planet as well as that of the mangled body of Flotilla-Leader Anderson, the man whose Plan they were using and who had been solidly behind Warren and the Escape until he discovered that it would entail the destruction of the town which had been named after him. And he could not in justice bawl out the Lieutenant because Warren himself shared much of the responsibility for the tragedy. How many times recently had he stated that they must stop at nothing to ensure the success of the Escape . . .?

'I'm sorry about this, too,' said Warren dully. He was silent for a moment, thinking. The Escape *had* to come off, to make all the unpleasant and inhuman things which were happening these days worthwhile, and to make sure that they did not happen again. Then briskly, he said, 'I take it this thing is not yet general knowledge?'

'The hunting party won't talk, sir,' said Kelso, looking relieved.

'And dead men and Staff officers don't tell tales,' Hutton added cynically.

'I'm sorry,' said Kelso, looking at everyone in turn. 'Really I am.'

Warren shook his head. 'It can't be helped. We must

expect casualties on an operation of this size and complexity, casualties not directly caused by enemy action——'

'Speaking of incidental casualties, sir,' Fielding broke in smoothly, but still looking daggers at Kelso, 'Lieutenant Nicholson complains that her girls going to and from duty at the hospital are being molested by——'

That was as far as she got before Sloan and Kelso shouted her down. Sloan's language was unsuitable for any company, mixed or otherwise, so that it was Kelso's relatively quiet voice which came through when the other had run out of profanity....

'... And this isn't a Sunday school outing we've planned!' the Lieutenant said furiously. 'It's a major operation, part of the *war*! I say these men deserve to get drunk or have sing-songs or play rough—they deserve all the fun they can get, because an awful lot of them won't be alive three weeks from now! They're going to take that ship with suits which are little short of death-traps. I say that with all respect for Major Hutton, who has done wonders with the what little he had to work with, but they are still death-traps. He's given us the means of carrying out a successful assault, but with an estimated loss due to component failure—suit failure, remember, not enemy action! —of sixty per cent...!'

He waved down Hutton's protest with a gesture which was definitely insubordinate and went on passionately, 'The men know these odds, they know why we've trained and equipped four times the number of officers needed for the job! Knowing these odds they still want to take part, would consider it a personal tragedy if they were not allowed to do so.

'They are a very special group of officers,' he rushed on, 'hand-picked for qualities of bravery, aggressiveness and toughness. Major Fielding as well as yourself, sir, went through their dossiers. Some of the officers here don't seem to realize what a really tremendous thing we're doing. This escape will go down in history, and *nothing* is too good for the officers who have the most difficult and dangerous part in it. To my mind, hampering the work with petty complaints and criticisms is little short of treason...!'

'Some of the girls,' growled Sloan suddenly, 'were just asking for it.'

Fielding swung furiously on him. 'Really, Major!' she said. 'You might like to know that one of the case histories I read mentioned severe concussion, caused by a blow from a not too blunt instrument which also necessitated major suturing of the scalp. Presumably the officer in question was playing hard to get. Or is it simply that our gallant assault officers—I hesitate to use the expression "officers and gentlemen"—have regressed to the point where they must use cave-man methods of courtship . . .?'

'Environmental influences, Major Fielding,' Hynds put in, his expression dead-pan. 'It comes from too much swinging about in trees . . .'

'That's enough!' said Warren sharply, as Kelso and Sloan opened their mouths for a return blast. He went on, 'We all deplore these incidents, naturally, but at the present time I can understand the feelings of Sloan and Kelso. All these officers know that they are expendable and that the greater number of them will be expended, so that the increasing strain they are under calls for our sympathy rather than for disciplinary action. We must try to retain our sense of proportion about this, weighing the relatively minor sufferings against the major achievement we hope to gain.

'I have devoted much thought to the final choosing of these assault groups,' Warren continued, trying to inject a lighter note into the proceedings, 'and it is unfortunate that a certain lack of charm is a concomitant of the other qualities I sought—but then who ever heard of a polite commando? We might all feel better if we remember that we're fighting a war, and think of all the people we've been discussing as casualties . . .'

As his eyes moved from face to face, Warren was becoming aware that his Staff was split down the middle, with Kelso, Sloan and himself ranged against Fielding, Hutton and Hynds. He knew that with each successive meeting the rift would widen and that in time he would have an open mutiny on his hands. The question was, how much time?

Could he hold them all together, and retain their loyalty and active support, for another three weeks . . .?'

CHAPTER SIXTEEN

Implacably, E-Day moved from the minus Twenties into the low 'teens. Two practice trips with battler-wagons and ships had been completed within their time schedules and without incident, the wild battlers who would be most likely to cause the incidents having been rendered virtually extinct by Sloan's hunters. The sections of the dummy were ready to go, the ambush tunnels were a few days off completion and the areas for destruction by fire and explosives were being marked out.

The many accidents and set-backs which occurred were of a minor nature and were directly ascribable to nerves in one form or another. There had been no further acts of sabotage.

On Minus Twelve Warren was working with Fielding on the evacuation of injured from the Escape area when she said suddenly, 'I don't like what the Escape has done to some of the people here, sir. I especially don't like what it has done to you. In my opinion you should slap an indefinite Hold on it—with a series of small delays to begin with, of course, so as to allow the Committee time to unwind—and start work on an alternative solution. It would be much better, sir, to found a dynasty . . .'

If there had been anyone else present Warren would have silenced such seditious talk at once, but they had known each other and served together so long that all he could do was grunt disapprovingly.

'On *Victorious* I was the only unmarried female officer,' she went on seriously, apparently changing the subject. 'As an unattached female who was also well-stacked I kept the other girls from taking their men too much for granted— potentially I was the Other Woman for the whole ship— and as the doctor-psychologist, again female, I served many of the functions of a mother as well. You, sir, with your absolute authority combined with the ease with which you could be approached, not to mention the concern you displayed for the safety of the officers serving under you, were the great granddaddy of all Father figures.

'Even in these decadent times,' she went on, holding his eyes steadily but with her face growing redder by the second, 'mothers and fathers are not infrequently married. To each other, I mean . . .'

Warren gaped at her, unable to speak.

'This, sir,' she said, lowering her eyes, 'is not a rhetoric proposal.'

A part of Warren's mind seemed to be chasing itself into a tight circle of confusion while another and less chaotic segment remembered a sunlit observation platform in their first Post. On that occasion Warren had considered long and deeply this alternative solution, and rejected it as being too uncertain. One of the reasons then for its rejection had been his own advanced age, but this particular reason no longer seemed quite so valid after three years of healthy, open air and virtually primitive living conditions. Those same conditions had done a lot for Ruth Fielding, too, Warren told himself as he tried not to look directly at her tight bolero jacket and even tighter pants, although in her case it was an improvement on near perfection.

He had to remind himself forcibly that the no longer valid reason had been a minor one in any case, and that all the other reasons still stood.

'I'm pretty sure the Escape will succeed, sir,' she went on suddenly, 'but I wonder sometimes if our people back home are really capable of mounting the rescue operation. I realize that you are more aware of the overall tactical situation than any of us here, but your information is three years old——'

'We have to escape!' said Warren harshly.

Until she had begun to talk again Warren's mind had been very far away indeed from the Escape. He had been thinking that aboard *Victorious* some things had been neither possible nor desirable. A female ship's Doctor-Psychologist was normally kept too busy seeing that everyone else was happy to have any time to feel unhappy herself—if the officer was as dedicated as Fielding, that was. And while ship marriage was the norm on active service, it was not supposed to be entered into between such widely disparate ranks as a Major and a Sector Marshal! In order to attain such eminence an officer had to devote all his mental and physical energy to his career, and it was assumed that sheer force of habit would see to it that he continued this devotion to duty when the pinnacle of power had been reached. A Sector Marshal might very well be approachable and democratic and go through all the motions of being just one of the boys, but a girl might just as soon think of marrying God.

On the prison planet, however, the situation was not the same as aboard ship. Here a King could look at a sex kitten...

It was the sudden and surprising violence of the temptation, as if her words and her warm, vital presence had triggered off an emotional time-bomb within him, which had shaken Warren so badly and roughened his voice. That and a terrible, growing suspicion.

Still looking at the table top, she went on quietly, 'A female psychologist indulging in self-analysis on the subject of love is probably more than you could bear, sir. So let's just say that I've taken so many men apart mentally that my need is for one with very special qualities and attributes, one that I can truly look up to. One of these attributes need not necessarily be youth.'

'Major Fielding ... Ruth ...!' began Warren, and stopped. When he went on a few seconds later he tried to adopt an avuncular manner, but his voice was so strained that he hardly recognized it. He said, 'I think that I've just been handed the nicest compliment of my whole life, Ruth. But what you're suggesting isn't possible. You'd be much better advised using your feminine wiles on Hutton, who spends more time looking at you during Staff meetings these days than anything or anyone else ...'

When Major Fielding left a few minutes later her face had been stiff and unreadable. The thought came to him that perhaps she had been telling the truth about her feelings towards him, but he suppressed it with a violence which was close to panic. It was much better to think the other way, that he had just foiled the third and potentially the most damaging act of sabotage yet attempted.

The thought should have brought him joy ...

On Minus Ten he had to read the riot act to Major Hynds, who had been complaining bitterly that his job was strictly third leg, and tell him in no uncertain terms that it was vital that the prisoners were not allowed to forget any of their technical know-how—or anything at all, for that matter. He sent Hynds on a five-day trip to the other continent to check on the re-education programme on the same day that he sent Hutton off to check on practically everything else. If either officer suspected that he was pulling the old divide and rule gambit on them—splitting them up so that they would have no chance to unite in opposition to Kelso, Sloan and himself—there was nothing they could do about it. Major Fielding was angrily co-operative, and Warren could not be sure whether it was the anger of a woman scorned or a conspirator foiled. On Minus Eight he made it known for the first time that Majors Hutton, Hynds and Fielding would take no actual part in the assault, citing as his reason the necessity of leaving behind a nucleus of technical brains for a second attempt should this one fail. In his best dour old warrior's voice he said that he was banking on this one succeeding, and if it didn't he could not bear the thought of having to do it all again.

The news that he intended going up with them gave a tremendous boost to the morale of the assault groups, although when Fielding heard about it her anger towards him became overlaid with a quality which Warren suspected was clinical appraisal . . .

On Minus Seven the assault groups went gradually onto a low residue diet, so far as was possible with locally grown food, and they went off alcohol completely. Warren had let them know in no uncertain language that he didn't want to go storming any ramparts with officers who were blind drunk or hung over. Six and Five he spent chiefly in reassuring officers of various ranks and specialities that he *did* know how to handle himself in one of Hutton's wastebaskets, that, having listened to the same lectures as they had, he was familiar with Bug physiology and the layout of their guardship, and that he was not contemplating any stupid heroics because he was getting too old and stiff. In short, he told them, he did not intend taking any risks and he was simply going along for the ride.

When they heard that, some of them tried to tell him how they felt. Awkwardly—even Kelso stumbled at it and Sloan was actually shy—they told him that he had done some highly peculiar things, almost suspicious things, in the past, but they knew now that he was with them and they were with him, no matter what. But the way they looked at him while they were talking made Warren feel even worse, because he had never been completely honest with any of them at any time.

In the late evening of Minus Four a top priority signal arrived from one of the observation posts on the eastern tip of the continent, which was already in darkness, saying that a Bug ship of the cruiser or small transport class was locked onto the guardship. It had arrived during daylight when the guardship was above the horizon and hence visible from the ground. Then four hours later, although both ships were by then well within the planetary shadow, the tail-flare of the cruiser illuminated the scene as it pulled away from the guardship preparatory to going into hyperdrive.

There could be no doubt as to what it all meant.

'What a blasted inconvenient time for them to land prisoners!' said Kelso, considerably understating Warren's own feelings in the matter. He added, 'If they follow the usual procedure, sir, we can expect the shuttle early tomorrow morning.'

Warren said, 'It would help to have some up-to-date intelligence about the crew and organization of the guardship, and the war, too, of course—but not if it means a Hold to get it. See that the prisoners are rounded up and interrogate as soon as possible, Lieutenant.'

The Bug shuttle landed on Minus Three at the time, but not in the place expected. It used exactly the same landing spot as had been used on its previous visit, and it delayed several minutes so that the new prisoners could get clear of its tail-flare before it took off—a clear indication that the Bugs were growing careless or else feeling less nervous about the possibility of an ambush by prisoners. Either way it was to Warren's advantage. The new arrivals were contacted and the position explained to them in double quick time—all except one, that was.

Hynds, back from the other continent and somewhat happier now that he had Intelligence work to do instead of acting like a glorified school inspector, made the report.

'It's difficult to process the men properly in the time allowed, sir,' he said briskly, 'but it seems clear that they are no great shakes mentally, unobservant to an amazing degree and shockingly uninformed regarding the overall tactical position. The forty-three prisoners landed represent the survivors of thirteen ships and actions fought over a period of three years, and many of them have spent this time being moved about from ship to ship as if the Bugs did not quite know what to do with them. From this we might infer that the Bug military organization is beginning to go rapidly to pieces, and I'm sure the missing officer would corroborate this if we could find him.

'I'm told that he is some kind of psychologist,' Hynds continued, 'and that he outranked the Captain of his ship, which was a heavy cruiser. I've had gliders and search parties out since the guardship set, but we haven't found him.'

'Fleet-Commander Peters,' said Kelso suddenly, 'has his farm in that area.'

In spite of himself Warren laughed. 'I don't think the Commander could do much to stop us, Lieutenant. Not with one convert, in three days . . .' He turned abruptly to Hynds. '. . . Better call in the search parties and gliders, Major. If he hasn't heard all that whistling and drumming or seen a plane and made a signal to it, a stray battler must have got him. And would you pass the word to Major Hutton—I think he's in number Two Attack Point—to meet me at the grenade store in forty-five minutes . . .'

Three. Two. One . . .

Ponderous, faultless and by now unstoppable, the vast machinery of the Escape rolled on. Holding as it did a thirty-two-and-a half hour orbit, which was the rotational period of the Bug home world, the guardship was below the horizon for just over sixteen hours. But in actual fact the Committeemen had closer to nineteen hours freedom from observation because they had been careful to choose for their surface transport routes which were well-sheltered by natural features—nearby hills and mountains, dense forest and the concealment afforded by the guardship's acute angle of observation through the atmospheric haze. At the present time, four hours after sunrise on E-minus One, the Bug ship was due to set in a little over three hours. In a very short time—Warren had to allow for possible delays in transmission—he could signal the final Go.

From Nicholson's post, which was almost deserted now since it, too, was due for destruction, the town and bay looked peacefully and unremarkably busy in the early sunlight. But there was a growing commotion outside his office, with voices raised so loudly in argument that two of them were recognizable. So he was not completely surprised when Sloan conducted Fleet-Commander Peters and a stranger into his presence.

'I expected to find you at the Escape site,' said Peters breathlessly, while Sloan was still opening his mouth. 'We've wasted far too much time. I've got to speak to you, sir. Alone . . .'

Warren didn't reply at once. Instead he examined the stranger from head to toe, seeing a small, overweight individual with a furiously sweating face whose expression reflected anxiety and confusion. Remembering his own feelings on being first pitchforked into the Committee–Civilian ideological conflict Warren felt a touch of sympathy for the man, but it was a very light and fleeting touch. He nodded for Sloan to wait outside, then turned to Peters.

'Go ahead, Commander,' he said.

Peters had recovered his breath but for some reason seemed to be finding it difficult to speak, and his eyes as they met Warren's held an expression which was very close to pity.

'I'm afraid you'll have to call it off, sir,' he said finally. 'You've no choice. The war is over . . .'

CHAPTER SEVENTEEN

'My name is Hubbard, sir,' the new man put in in a nervous jerky voice. 'Political Officer from the late *Resolution*. It isn't over, exactly—but it amounts to the same thing. Neither side has the resources, technical, material or personnel, to go on with it ...!'

'Political Officer?' asked Warren dully. It was a completely new rank to him, and even though he felt that the planet had just been pulled from under his feet the process of satisfying his curiosity was automatic.

The position had been created because of the growing distrust of field commanders by High Command, Hubbard explained, the situation being aggravated by the accelerating breakdown of all military organization and communications. In part this was due to the incredibly poor quality of present officer material, it being the accepted thing these days to refuse rather than to force battle with the enemy. The men just would not fight— although in honesty Hubbard said that this was due to distrust of their own ships and equipment as much as inner qualms. Despite this the officers on space service had been built up as heroes by home propaganda in an attempt to boost the war effort, and this had given some of the field commanders a very nice idea.

Not just as single ships but in flotillas and whole Sector subfleets they had simply opted out of the war. But they had not gone home. Instead they had taken themselves to some of the colony worlds—planets with small populations and light defences—and as heroes placed their worlds under their protection. Or held them to ransom, or tried to carve small, personal empires out of them, depending on the characteristics of the commander concerned and the number of units he possessed whose captains were personally loyal to him. It was Hubbard's duty, and the duty of the other political officers serving with the remains of the fleet, constantly to remind the ships' personnel where their true loyalty lay, because not only the military organization but the whole of Earth's interstellar culture was rapidly falling to pieces. And it was no comfort at all to know that the Bugs were having the same trouble . . .

'. . . The Fleet Commander has told me what you're trying to do and I think it's tremendous!' Hubbard rushed on. 'But it is a complete waste of lives and effort, sir, believe me. What remains of our military organization is scarcely capable of mounting an offensive patrol much less a rescue operation for the rest of the prisoners! You've got a nice, tight organization here, sir. You'd be better advised to stay put and——'

'Peters,' said Warren suddenly, 'how many people know about this?'

The Fleet Commander smiled. He said, 'Give me credit for a little intelligence, sir. Nobody but ourselves. Releasing it to your people in their present frame of mind would not be smart. I thought you had better handle it, break it to them gently after a long series of Holds . . .'

'Sloan!'

The Major charged into the room, his cross-bow unslung and ready, eyes glaring. Harshly, Warren said, 'Put these men under close arrest. They are not to be allowed to speak. They are to be confined separately so that they cannot attempt subversion by talking to each other and allowing their seditious talk to be overheard. They are not to say "Good Morning" or "Thank you" when meals are served. If they utter one word they are to be killed.'

'Yes, *sir*!' said Sloan.

'You . . . you can't,' began Peters incredulously. 'You're mad, *power* mad . . .!'

The words were choked off as in response to Warren's nod Sloan brought up his weapon, aimed at the centre of the Commander's forehead and pulled the trigger. The bolt thudded into a log two feet above the Commander's head because at the penultimate instant Warren had used the heel of his hand to jar the Major's elbow.

'You are not to speak at all,' he said quietly. 'Is that understood?'

It was understood.

Second thoughts and last minute changes of plan were

dangerous, Warren told himself firmly, and a decision taken calmly and unhurriedly should not be altered because of them—especially if they arose because of cowardice, selfishness or the possibility of taking an easy way out. But he gave the final Go signal within minutes of Peters and Hubbard being marched out because he did not want to give himself time to think anyway . . .

The last few yards of the main tunnel was opened to the surface while the wooden framework of the dummy was going up around it. These massive, hoop-like sections—prefabricated, numbered for ease of assembly and stored in town many months previously—were rushed out to the Escape site by gangs of as many as twenty men to each section. Their route was a straight line from town to the site, but no attempt was made to conceal their tracks in the soft earth because it would later be burned over to look like the scar of a C-7 blast. And while the framework was being assembled, at a pace which could only be described as furious despite the frequent measurement checks, smaller parties were carefully setting alight to the farmhouse which was supposed to be burned by the force-landed ship and to the trees and undergrowth sheltering the two forward attack points.

These positions had to appear to be razed to the ground, but at the same time the scorched tree-trunks, bushes and log walls had to give concealment to a large number of men. While this carefully supervised destruction was going on, survey teams with mirrors, flags and extremely loud voices were checking on the alignment of trees in the sections due for burning. Some were marked down for fire-paste and others, those nearest the site, to be blown down with explosive while literally thousands of small trees and bushes had sheets of paper impaled and tied onto a conspicuous branch in such a way that they would burn off but not blow off in a wind, and these were to be ignited by torch. Simultaneously the grass and brush and the more inflammable species of tree along the edges of the fire lanes were being wetted down with water carried from the bay, the marsh or the nearby stream. Some of it had to be carried, in great hide gourds slung on poles, for more than three miles.

On no account could the conflagration so soon to take place to be allowed to get out of control, to look like an ordinary, naturally occurring forest fire . . .

And through the smoke haze from the burning farm the helio on Nicholson's post blinked out a constant stream of progress reports. The dummy's section had left its mountain and was half-way to the coast. The stabilizers were twenty minutes behind it. The last of the hull sections had left Hutton's Mountain. Weather forecast was for no change in wind velocity or direction, but there was a possibility of cloud around dawn. Hutton was having trouble with a temperamental battler at the head of his convoy and was twenty-five minutes behind schedule. Hutton had turned the battler loose and was having its load pulled by the extra men he had brought along for just this contingency. The lock sections had been loaded onto their cat and it was at sea, winds favourable. Hutton had picked up ten minutes by Johnson's Bridge, and it was observed that he was helping to pull the lead wagon. A small cat fleet had rendezvoused at Chang's Inlet and the smaller metal sections dispersed among the cliff caves there were being ferried out to them. One of the boats had capsized in the shallows. Its load had been dragged ashore and transferred to another boat—estimated delay forty-five minutes. The first cat was hull up on the horizon. The head of Hutton's convoy was now five hours away . . .

The helio stopped blinking because the sun was suddenly down among the trees. There was a perhaps an hour of usable dusk left, then the remainder of the work would have to be done by torchlight. The signals were resumed, using a focussed oil-lamp and shutter. With a red-orange light which gave overtones of anger to everything it said, Nicholson's post gave the news that the guardship would rise in eight hours and seventeen minutes . . .

By the light of bonfires and strategically placed torches the lock and stabilizer sections were fitted, the tanks of Bug air were brought up and positioned inside the framework and the periscopes were set up and aligned. The vanguard of Hutton's convoy came rumbling and creaking onto the Escape site, off-loaded hurriedly because the fires were making the battlers restive, and returned to town. While their load of metal plating was being lifted, manhandled into positions and hung onto their proper place on the framework, the empty wagons were reloaded with furniture, personal possessions and litters for the injured and driven to the other side of town where they were parked by the roadside. There they waited, just as the cats in the bay were waiting—although in their case the furniture and sundry oddments were carried mainly to break up or hide the outlines of the deck cargo of dismantled gliders and similar items too valuable to be destroyed with the town.

It was like a scene from some surrealist's Hell, with red-eyed, smoke-blacked demons aswarm over an alien and uncompletable jig-saw puzzle in three dimensions. But they were completing it—all the pieces had reached the site and smooth metal flesh was growing across the bare bones of the dummy. And so far everything had gone without a hitch.

Something should go wrong, Warren felt, something serious. But nothing did.

Men fell or burned themselves with torches or had heat-stroke or had members crushed during the process of assembly or while unloading wagons. They were taken to the hospital in town and then to the litter wagons. But these were only minor hitches, the ones which had been planned for. Just as was the fact that they were still a little behind schedule.

'The discharge of a C-7 is detectable at line of sight,' Warren said worriedly, and unnecessarily, to Hutton. 'We have to light the fires at least an hour before the guardship clears the horizon or they'll know it isn't the right thing.'

'Just three more sections to go, sir!' said Hutton, the smoke, excitement and the strain of too much shouting all contributing to the hoarseness of his voice. 'They're at ground level and won't give much trouble, and we'll have them in position before the heat and smoke gets too bad. So you can give the signal now, sir . . .!'

Hutton's face and body were so thickly caked with soot, sweat and grime that he had the aspect of a piece of smoke-blackened sculpture, but the excited, shining eyes and the even brighter gleam of teeth were not the expressions of a thing of stone. Grinning in return, Warren slipped the lanyard of his whistle over his head and handed it to the Major.

'*You* give the signal,' he said.

There was a moment of absolute quiet after the high, clear note of the whistle sounded, then the silence was broken by more whistles, shouted orders and sporadic cheering punctuated by the thud of explosions and the angry hiss of fire-paste. At a few widely separate points around the site a red glow showed through the trees a few sparks drifted into the air, but as yet there was not much to see.

'I want to get a better view of all this,' Warren said briskly, turning to enter the dummy. He passed, patted the smooth metal plating beside him and added, 'You've done a good job, Major, a very good job. When assembly is complete, leave—there's nothing more for you to do here. Go help Fielding with the road evacuation, she might want you to pull a wagon or something. And, uh, look after her, Major. Give us time to reach the guardship, then ... Well, what you do after that depends on circumstances, but whatever happens you are going to have an awful lot to do.'

'I understand,' said Hutton in a low voice. His eyes were not shining quite so brightly and his teeth did not show at all. He went on, 'If you don't ... I mean, I can't be sure that I can organize a second Escape. The way things are at the moment, sir, I couldn't promise——'

'And I wouldn't want you to, Major,' said Warren meaningfully, even though he knew that at present the meaning was lost on Hutton.

'Good luck, sir,' said the Major.

Warren went through the opening in the dummy's hull, around or under the timber braces and into the mouth of the main ambush tunnel. The compartments opening off it were full of men checking weapons or airtanks or just sitting quietly beside their spacesuits. One of the rooms, the testing compartment, was full of deep and very muddy water and another was festooned with as yet unclaimed spacesuits, one of which was his own. At the other end of the tunnel the road was becoming well-lit by the growing number of fires, and he made good time to the town and to

126

the harbour. The glider refused to unstick from the water until its rockets were almost burned out and they made only five hundred feet, but by then there was no dearth of warm updraughts of air to help them.

A very fine man, Major Hutton, Warren thought; *the type of personality and mind which should be preserved, no matter what the cost!* The thought gave him a little comfort, although it could not make him completely sure that what he was doing was right . . .

From two thousand feet the scene resembled a tremendous wheel of fire whose hub was the blunt torpedo shape of the dummy and whose spokes radiated in lines of burning trees and vegetation to the Post, to the many farms up the valley and to the town. Around the site the greenery gave off much smoke and burned with a loud frying sound. But most of the spokes radiated towards the town, and here the wooden buildings were dry and roared and they burned and hurled clouds of sparks half a mile into the air.

It looked both spectacular and highly artificial. Satisfied, Warren tapped his pilot's shoulder and they dived through the smoke and sparks towards a landing in the bay.

They put Warren into his suit then. After the freedom and comfort of a kilt the battledress part alone felt hot and constricting, and when they fitted the wickerwork shield, helmet and airtanks he felt even worse. As respectfully as possible in the circumstances, they held him head downwards in the muddy pool of water so that they could check the seal between issue battledress and home-made helmet. He was dunked three times before he was able to tell them where the water was coming through.

A wide leather strap laterally encircled his head and served to anchor a large sponge pad to his forehead. A second strap going around the top of his head and under his chin held the first one in place and gave support to yet another strap, a thin one this time, which crossed just under his nose. To this one was attached a thin, hollow cane, and when they took him out of the pool and laid him face down he worked his lips about until the cane was between his teeth and then drank the muddy water. There was about half a pint of the stuff.

Water inside the helmet during weightless manoeuvring

could be deadly, and drinking it was the only way of getting rid of it. He was helped to his feet, motioned to crane his neck forward so as to wipe away the remaining droplets with his forehead pad, then assisted towards the dummy along the tunnel which was now lined with space-suited figures resting against nearly vertical planks. Their eyes followed him as he passed, caught by the big numeral '1' painted on his wickerwork shield, and under the ludi-crous nose-strap and drinking straw gadgets their teeth showed in a smile. Warren stopped long enough at each one of them to tap out 'Good Luck' against their face-pieces, show his own teeth and wag an admonishing finger if any one of them started to come to attention.

Kelso and Sloan were already in the dummy, propped in their wooden supports near one of the periscopes, waiting. Warren joined them.

CHAPTER EIGHTEEN

After having had the fires under observation during dark-ness, when they would have been seen to the best advan-tage, and having drawn certain conclusions from these observations, it was expected that the Bugs would send down a probe for a closer look. Instead of a quick dive in and out of the atmosphere, which was the usual procedure when investigating any suspicious occurrence, it was ex-pected that curiosity would make them soft-land the probe for a really close look. And it was known that if the vehicle landed it would not have enough fuel left to return to the guardship. Being an extremely valuable piece of equipment, the Bugs would not soft-land it in the first place unless they expected to get it back. The only way they could do that was to bring it back aboard the shuttle, and if they con-sidered landing the shuttle they could not be feeling too suspicious.

The probe arrived about two hours before noon. On the way down it had a perfect view of cats hurrying out of the bay, many of which were towing rafts; of the refugees on wagons and afoot, well advanced along all the roads leading from the town; of the town itself, devastated and still burning in many places, its gutted corpse hidden by a filthy shroud of smoke. It could see the acres of smouldering tree stumps and vegetation, and the highly-unnatural outline of the destruction which proved that a weapon designed for use over a range of thousands of miles of vacuum was capable of wreaking considerable havoc despite the blanketing effects of atmosphere.

It noted the ship crash-landed and toppled on to its side, observing and relaying back the fine details of the buckled stabilizer which must have given on landing, the partly open airlock and sprung plating which steamed faintly with escaping chlorine, and the slit in the nose where the C-7 blister hadn't closed properly. And there was the smoking remains of the farmhouse close by, whose occupants were no doubt the indirect cause of the surrounding devastation, which had been set on fire by its tail-flare.

So far the data was simply corroborative material for the telescopic observers in the guardship. But suddenly the probe opened out like a flower with super-sensitive vision, sound and analysis equipment, in effect subjecting the area to a microscopic as well as a telescopic examination.

Such an examination could not be allowed to continue.

A lone figure came staggering out of a patch of un-burned vegetation some fifty yards from the probe. His body was terribly burned and bleeding from wounds inflicted by sharp branches, even his leather harness was charred and cracked by the heat, and from his mouth there came a steady, high-pitched moaning that was a continuous low scream. He carried a club in the shape of a heavy table-leg, and when he saw the landed probe he screamed harshly and came stumbling towards it.

In actual fact Briggs was suffering no discomfort at all. His ghastly appearance was due solely to imaginative make-up, his club was a very carefully fashioned table-leg weighted and balanced to inflict the maximum damage, and he had landed one of the easiest jobs in the whole operation simply through his acting ability. He was supposed to disable the probe so that the Bugs would be thrown back on to the resources of the telescopes on the ship and their own, unaided eyesight when they landed later—if they landed later. So dutifully, almost gleefully, Briggs set about battering the probe into scrap, hamming the part of a poor, pain-crazed prisoner for all he was worth.

But he must have been a little too enthusiastic in his use of the club. The battering must have opened a path between the probe's fuel tank and the still red-hot venturis. There could only have been a few ounces of fuel remaining in the tank, but it was enough. There was a sudden flare, a concussion which made the whole dummy jerk around him, and when he reached the periscope Warren could see that there was very little left of Briggs or the probe.

Warren settled back for another period of waiting, and thinking.

Vitally important, but safe, was how Warren had described the assignment to Briggs. The probe should be given just enough time to report on the desolation around the site, the absence of any possibly dangerous groups of prisoners, of harmful activity, of anything except burning, smouldering vegetation and a ship which had crash-landed and was leaking chlorine. Then it would have to be disabled so that the small sounds made by the hidden assault groups would not be picked up. It was not expected that the Bugs would booby-trap the probe, since it would be much simpler to drop a bomb on the area if their suspicions were aroused. Briggs had agreed that all this was so, and his expression had reminded Warren of the time when this same Briggs had shown him how to swing a hammock where the battlers couldn't reach it and Warren had nearly hung himself on the safety rope—the expression of a man trying hard not to laugh . . .

The time dragged past and the sun beat down on the site and on the metal dummy. Inside the dummy the heat was unbearable and inside the suits it was even worse. Kelso, Sloan and himself were now lying prone with a suit technician attending each of them. The technician had removed the gauntlet sections of the battledress and placed their hands in small pans of water, indicating that they should lift them in and out at intervals. He also kept wetting down the accessible portions of their fish-bowls. Evaporation from their hands and helmets was supposed to cool them and avoid heat-stroke, but Warren was convinced that the water treatment's effect was chiefly psychological.

Above them, invisible in the sunshine, the Bugs should have made their decision—the only decision possible to them if they had any decent feelings at all. The accidental destruction of their probe should not have aroused suspicion, considering the circumstances, and the shuttle should already be on the way down to rescue the survivors of the crash-landed ship—some of whom *must* be alive to judge by the the devastation surrounding it! But something *might* have made them suspicious, or perhaps they were too cowardly to send a rescue party, and a missile was on the way down instead to ensure that one of their ships did not fall into the hands of the prisoners . . .

Suddenly the suit technician waved and pointed upwards, but it was not until Warren reached the periscope that the sound of the shuttle coming down got through his helmet. He didn't see the landing because of the smoke and ash being blown through the gap in the plating where the periscope was set up, but he could tell that it was very close, and the elation he felt was due only in part to the beautiful way things were working out. A contributory factor was his knowledge that, not soon but in the foreseeable future, he would be able to get out of the pressure-cooker he was using for a spacesuit . . . !

The clouds of smoke from the many small fires started by the landing served to hide the movements of the ground assault men, from the eyes on the ship as well as those in space, as they took up their positions in the unburned cover around the edge of the Escape site. Some small trees fell, stirring up more smoke. In actual fact they were being pushed over and damp grass and twigs at hand for the purpose were being used to produce smoke—the idea being to accustom the Bug rescuers to falling trees and sudden, dense clouds of smoke. They might be frightened by these effects, but the whole area was smouldering and constantly being re-ignited by sudden puffs of wind—so that they should not be suspicious of them. And when the smoke was allowed to clear temporarily the shuttle could be seen standing about one hundred yards from the dummy with the burned farmhouse almost directly between them.

It wasn't an ideal position for the ambush, Warren thought, but it could have been much worse.

With gestures which were an improbable combination of salute, cheery wave and thumbs-up sign, Kelso and Sloan disappeared into the mouth of the tunnel heading for Number Two Attack Point, which was very nearly to windward of the shuttle's position and from which the main body of commandos would be able to approach the ship under cover of smoke. At Warren's signal the suit technician stopped pouring water over him and began pounding on the interior of the metal hull with a piece of wood. It was a slow, irregular beat, not very loud but still capable of being heard all over the Escape site, and it was the sort of noise which might very well be made by someone trying to attract attention when radio or other means of communication was impossible. That would be how the Bugs in the shuttle would regard it, Warren told himself. And later, if the pounding should vary in beat or volume they should regard it as a sign of impatience or desperation on the part of the survivor and not as instructions going out to the assault groups via drum-talk . . .

The shuttle's lock swung suddenly open and the ladder with its oddly-shaped rungs and stubby handrail came telescoping down. A billow of smoke from the fires behind Number Two rolled past the enemy ship and when it cleared there were two Bugs on the ladder. A few seconds later there were four, all descending as quickly as was possible for that particular life-form to move. Excitement as well as heat made Warren's mouth go dry.

They intended making a fast rescue. That much was plain from the speed of their descent and the fact that the cargo lock remained sealed—they weren't going to break out one of their ground vehicles. And the normal crew of the shuttle was three. Counting the one they must have left on radio watch there were five beings in the rescue party, which was a further indication that they suspected nothing or they would not have risked so many at one time. But the four Bugs moving away from the base of the landing ladder were armed—they might not be suspicious but at the same time neither were they stupid. In addition they carried metal-cutting equipment and packs which probably contained medication of some kind, all hung from the light-weight type of suit which gave the maximum amount of physical mobility with, as was usual with such suits, the minimum of physical protection. All at once Warren felt sorry for them.

From the Bug point of view this was simply an errand of mercy, but one which required a considerable amount of intestinal fortitude to carry out. To eyes accustomed to much higher light intensities the Escape site must appear a very spooky place. Even though the sun shone through an obscuring cloud of smoke, the light was not good. All around them the ground smouldered, rendering objects and distances uncertain in what must appear to be a hot and foggy twilight, and when a large cloud of smoke drifted past their visibility would drop to a few yards. People who would subject themselves to such conditions, even for a few minutes, possessed qualities which Warren could admire. It was a pity that these admirable qualities would serve only to get their possessors killed in a few minutes from now.

Warren signalled again and the technicians gave the hull a single, solid blow which made the interior of the dummy ring like a discordant gong. In the distance there was the crash of falling trees and the soft crackling of fires, both too far away to seriously frighten the Bugs. Behind Warren the smoke aimed at screening the site from the guardship's tele-scopes, which at that time were thirty-two degrees above the horizon with a thickening atmospheric haze to pene-trate in addition to the smoke pall, was rising like a thick, blue fog. At the same time Number Two were busily mak-ing smoke which rolled slowly towards the shuttle, billow-ing upwards as it came to drift past the control-room ports high in the ship's nose. At ground level this smoke appeared to be clotted here and there, but even to Warren's more sensitive human vision the wavering, indistinct shadows did not at all resemble a slow-walking file of men.

One to get ready . . . he thought.

As a species the Bugs were six-limbed and insect-like, but lacking in the protective carapace or ⋅ exo-skeleton developed by many Earth insects—they were the type of bug which squished rather than cracked when it was walked on. Their bodies seemed altogether too soft and heavy for their four walking legs, mainly because of the high liquid content of their systems and the fact that the movement of each vital organ or muscle was reflected as a constant twitching and bubbling of their semi-transparent teguments. But they were in no sense physical weaklings. Their two manipulators which projected forwards from each side of the head section, which in turn was connected to the main body by a short and ridiculously thin neck, were both sensitive and immensely strong. The manipulators, mouth and general sensory equipment housed in the head section had the hairy, frond-like appearance of something which might have been grown under the sea. Not all of these physical details were visible as the four Bugs rounded the farmhouse, but because they were wearing the equivalent of the tight-fitting service battledress there was very little hidden.

Two to get set . . .

The second gong-like note made them hesitate, as did the realistic collapse of one wall of the farmhouse with the accompanying dense smoke. But they came on, their bodies wobbling like water-filled balloons in their haste, their head sections swaying heavily from side to side. Behind the dummy the smoke was rising so high and becoming so thick that the whole Escape site was darkened. The Bugs were now hidden from sight of the shuttle by the ruined farmhouse. They came to a halt before the dummy's air-lock, and one of them suddenly began to move away again, obviously intending to have a look at the other side of the mock-up. Warren made frantic chopping motions with his hand.

. . . And three to GO!

The reverberating of the final signal and the subsidence of more wreckage from the farmhouse both served to keep Warren from hearing the twang of cross-bows from the farmhouse, from points all around the site and from positions further along the interior of the dummy. It seemed suddenly as if the four Bugs had grown bristles—thick and very short bristles, because the bolts had penetrated deeply. They rolled over soggily and lay still, leaking the yellow stuff they used for blood and which turned black within a few seconds of being exposed to the oxygen-laden air.

Warren swung away from the periscope and hurried carefully towards the airlock, thinking that if the four Bugs had made any noise as they died, which was very unlikely, the one left aboard the shuttle might put it down to a cry of surprise at the sudden cave-in of wreckage, some of which might have fallen too close for comfort.

The Bug in the ship could not suspect anything yet, but it would require only a few minutes of not being able to raise its friends on their suit radios for it to become very anxious indeed. What happened after that depended on how well the Bug could see, how easily it became confused and, most important of all, how many fine and admirable qualities it possessed.

The dummy's airlock dropped open and Warren went through it, running.

CHAPTER NINETEEN

Because the dummy was supposed to be lying on its side the lock's outer seal formed a short, steep ramp to the ground. Warren stumbled going down it and the sweat of fear was mixed briefly with the super-heated perspiration already bathing him as he thought of the possible effects of a fall on the too-brittle seals of his helmet and air-hose. But he recovered balance and ran carefully into the smoky sunshine of the site, rounding the farmhouse on the side opposite that used by the Bug rescue party and heading for the tall shadow in the smoke which was the shuttle. He was not running much risk of being seen because the Bug on watch, if it could see anything at all in the smoke, would be watching the place where its friends had last gone from sight.

Most of the assault force was already in position, packed tightly into the small circle around the ship's stern which was hidden from the control-room by the bulge of the hull. A few feet above their heads the flaring mouth of the main venturi, still glowing red, was a stark reminder of their fate should the Bug upstairs decide suddenly to take off. There were two figures already on the ladder, climbing rapidly and silently on padded boots—Kelso and Sloan were not wasting any time. Two other men, the pilots, were starting up the ladder as Warren reached it. He joined them, having to pull rank on the other commandos waiting to ascend by tapping a few helmets firmly and indicating the number painted on his shield. He mounted silently, although not as quickly as Kelso and Sloan, so that the only noise from the ladder was the regular tap, thump, tap-tap made by the Committeeman beating on one of the hand-rails with padded sticks.

Considerable research had gone into the development of that particular rhythm, which was the nearest they could come to the sound made by a six-limbed being slowly climbing a ladder. The Bug in the control-room should be really confused by that sound, since it had just seen its friends disappear towards the dummy and if any one of them had a reason for coming back it would have told him about it on the suit radio. The other possibility was that a survivor from the crashed ship had been wandering in the area and found its way to the shuttle, missing its four rescuers in the smoke. This was a pretty strong possibility, Warren told himself desperately, and even if the Bug was frightened it would think twice about taking off and abandoning its friends and this possible survivor. At this moment it was probably asking the advice of its superior in the guardship about the situation.

The first bolas with its attached line whirled upwards past Warren as he climbed, closely followed by two more, to wrap themselves around the thin metal post and spidery antenna which projected from the hull a few yards above the lock. The weights on each bolas were enclosed in padded bags to ensure maximum silence in use, and the bolas with its attached line had been soaked in a super-saturated solution of $CuSO_4$ until a few seconds before it was needed, and the other end of the wetted lines were being grounded in equally wet earth. Copper wire fine enough to be woven into a rope was beyond even Hutton's present resources, so that water and copper salts had had to serve instead.

The three lines tightened suddenly and Warren saw the antenna support quiver, bend slightly, then sag until it was lying almost flat against the hull.

If everything had worked as it should, the cutting off of communications between guardship and shuttle should not have been a dramatically sudden or frightening occurrence. There should have been a gradual fading of signal strength followed by a complete fade-out as the bolas first grounded the antenna and then pulled it off target, and the whole thing would be attributed to malfunctioning equipment—the other person's equipment, of course. They should not be suspicious. Warren told himself as he reached the top of the ladder, not yet . . .

The lock chamber was a large compartment extending deep into the ship, a three-way lock opening into the prisoner accommodation as well as the Bug-inhabited section. It allowed POWs to be disembarked without having to contaminate the whole ship with oxygen or letting the prisoners retain their complete spacesuits. The ship could carry up to one hundred prisoners in four closely-spaced decks connected by a ladder running up through a central well, so that the top two decks and the entire length of the ladder was covered by the weapon mounted in the floor of the control-room. This was an unsophisticated but very effective affair firing solid projectiles only, since anything more devastating might have blown the stern off the ship. The other seal opened into a companionway leading to the control-room, but in a series of flat zig-zags which was more comfortable for climbing by the ungainly Bug life-form. The two pilots were standing beside the Bug seal, and Warren joined them so as to avoid blocking the assault men who were silently following him up the ladder. Sloan was knocking the last of a series of wedges into the pivot of the outer seal, quietly with his fist. The metal wedges were padded for silence of insertion and for increased friction when in place. Kelso, a pouch of wedges tied to his middle, was checking the manual controls of the prison-deck seals.

In a war lasting as long as this one had, it was natural for both sides to gain knowledge of how and why each other's equipment worked, there being an ample number of wrecks to study. It was normal practice on both sides to have a manual over-ride on all lock controls, a local control which in turn could be over-ridden only by an Emergency Lock. But once the seals were opened on local and wedged, the emergency controls would not be able to close them. The snag was that the operation of the manuals would show on the control-room tell-tales.

There was about twenty men in the lock chamber now, standing motionless and with their wickerwork armours making them look like grotesque half-vegetables in the garish blue light used by the Bugs. The man at the base of the ladder had stopped reproducing Bug footsteps and the occupant of the control-room would be expecting this Bug-that-never-was to open one of the seals. Being a survivor of the crashed ship, and hence unfamiliar with the purpose of the shuttle, it was likely that it would open the larger of the two seals, the one leading into the POW quarters.

Kelso opened the large seal and sidled back along the wall to join Warren, Sloan and the pilots at the smaller one. The assault men crowding the compartment moved through and began to mount the ladder to the prison decks, their place being taken by men already on the landing ladder. In addition to cross-bows they carried bunches of long, thick canes which could be slotted and locked together to form a thirty-foot lance. With these metal-tipped lances it was hoped that the men could get high enough to damage the machine-gun projecting from the control-room blister, or even smash through the transparent plastic of the blister itself. It was possible, just barely conceivable, that they could storm the control-room with them. But the attack through the POW section was to be mainly diversionary . . .

It took about eight seconds after the large seal was opened for the Bug to react, then the machine-gun burped thunderously and two men crashed to the bottom of the ladder. One of them landed head first and he remained in that position, with one leg hooked around the fifth rung and his body held unnaturally stiff by his wickerwork shield, effectively blocking the ascent of the others. An officer bent forward to detach him from the ladder and continued to bend forward until he was flat on the deck, splinters flying from his back as a stream of metal tore through him. The same burst sent another man higher up the ladder crashing to the deck, and somehow the first officer's body was no longer blocking the way. The men in the lock compartment pressed forward again. None of them got higher than the third rung.

But still the men came crawling up the ladder from the ground and pushing past him, as if eager to get to some wild and wonderfully exclusive party. There must have been twenty or more bodies around the base of the ladder now, twitching and writhing feebly as they died from their wounds or from chlorine coming through smashed helmets, or from both. Many of them were plainly dead and moved only because the weapon above gave them no peace. And the whole horrible, twitching mass leaked red, a red that was too vivid and garish in the harsh blue light to look like blood.

Warren found himself pounding at Kelso's arm with his fist and shouting—to no avail since the words were inaudible in the din outside his own helmet—for the Lieutenant to get on with it! But Kelso refused to move until he was good and ready, which meant the next time there was a sustained burst of fire from the control-room. When that happened the Bug's eyes would be on its weapon and not on the master panel, where the opening to the second lock would be registering. He stopped maltreating Kelso's upper arm and forced himself to look at the slaughter again.

Somebody had got the bright idea of going up the ladder two at a time, one in the normal way and the other on the inside where it projected a couple of feet from the wall. The man on the inside had the ladder's supporting struts to climb around as well as mounting the rungs, but it was a very good idea. The first time it was tried a very long burst indeed was needed to pick the inside man off the ladder, and Warren was suddenly aware that the seal beside him was open and Kelso was thumping a wedge into place.

They went up the zig-zag companionway fast, but carefully so as not to spring a leak in their suits—Kelso, Sloan, the two pilots and Warren trying hard to keep up with the younger men. They had to reach the control-room before the Bug had time to think, time to realize that its friends were dead, that there were no survivors from a crash-landed ship and that the present attack was so well-timed that the whole thing had to be an elaborate ambush. They had to get there before it decided to hit the emergency take-off button. It could even wreck the Escape by putting an Emergency Lock on the air-tight hatch leading into the control-room, by making it impossible for Kelso to operate the manual controls . . .

But the hatch was wide open when they reached it, the big, circular cover standing at right angles to the control-room floor. Kelso banged home a wedge so enthusiastically that he overbalanced and just kept himself from falling by grabbing the edge of the opening with both hands. He was still hanging there and trying to get his feet back onto the companionway as Sloan carefully withdrew a heavily-padded bag from his pouch and from the bag took even more carefully a large, lumpy ovoid of glass. The glass container held nothing more harmful—to humans, that was—than oxygen under pressure, and the glass was much thinner than that used in the suit air-tanks. He lobbed the glass container into the control-room, waited for five seconds and then went charging up through the hatch with one of the pilots hot on his heels.

There was a soft, red explosion in the region of Sloan's stomach and the Major folded violently in the middle and rolled from sight. The pilot toppled backwards a second later, his helmet and head inside it blown open. The Bug up there had a side-arm, too, Warren thought sickly, of the type which fired explosive pellets. But the Bug had no business being alive, with an oxygen bomb bursting beside it . . . !

The second pilot was going up and Warren had to restrain him. He couldn't talk to the man, but by dint of hanging onto one of his arms and climbing above him he made the officer realize that the reason they'd had two

pilots was in case one had an accident, and since one of
them had had an accident the second pilot was no longer
expendable. By the time the other was convinced of this
Warren was himself part-way into the control-room and
the Bug was shooting at him. But Warren was still covered
by the upright hatch seal, which rang loudly with each hit
of an exploding pellet, and he was additionally fortunate in
that the Bug was trying to do two things and watch three
places at once.

One of its manipulators held the side-arm, the other
worked the machine-gun covering the prisoner well while
its head jerked heavily from the hatch to the machine-gun
to the control panel behind it and back to the hatch again.
A few feet from the Bug the oxygen bomb lay unbroken
where it had fallen into the deep padding of an acceleration
couch. Warren swore and flung his knife, but it didn't hit a
vital spot and it landed handle first anyway. He backed
away hurriedly, using the hatch for cover until a projecting
metal cabinet gave him slightly more protection.

Kelso's head rose suddenly above the rim of the opening,
and Warren began frantically drawing triangles in the air
with his fore-finger. Kelso's bewilderment was plain even
through the small area of helmet not covered by his
wickerwork.

A wedge! Warren screamed silently at him, trying by
sheer telepathy to make the other understand. *Something
hard and heavy to throw at that gas-bomb! A wedge, you
stupid idiot—a wedge with the padding off . . .!*

Looking puzzled, the Lieutenant began knocking another
wedge into the hinged side of the hatch cover.

Sloan was still moving. The Major was bumping himself
along the control-room deck like some grotesque snail, with
agonizing slowness, leaving a trail that was bright red
rather than silvery. He was not moving directly towards
the couch with the oxygen bomb on it or towards even the
Bug, but was instead inching along a course which could
only take him against the metal supports of the communications desk—perhaps he had no idea where he was going.
Despite the tight fit of the battledress suits, chlorine must be
already seeping into his helmet from the tear caused by the
pellet, and the Major's abdominal wound was the worst

141

thing Warren had ever seen in a life-time of war service. The Major was *dead*! Warren wished fervently that he would admit the fact and stop moving. But he did not stop until he bumped into the communications desk supports, and then he struggled and heaved weakly until he was on his side. Warren didn't see what he did then because for a few seconds he couldn't bear to look at him, but when he did look back Sloan was gripping one of the supports with both hands. With a sudden, convulsive effort the Major pulled the unprotected section of his helmet against the metal strut.

He must have opened his air taps because the contents of both his tanks went whistling out through his smashed helmet. The Bug jerked back, dropped its weapon and began tearing at its gills. Warren climbed to his feet and snatched up the unbroken gas-bomb and smashed it with totally unnecessary violence at the Bug's feet. It shrivelled visibly, wrapped its six limbs tightly around itself and died. Major Sloan had finally stopped moving, but somehow Warren could not stop looking at him.

He became aware suddenly of a lance smashing through the machine-gun blister and of cross-bow bolts smacking off the control-room ceiling. Of the pilot checking the positions of essential controls, and of Lieutenant Kelso tearing the padding off a wedge and handing it to him.

Warren took it and on the nearest bulkhead he hammered out the signal 'All Secure . . .'

CHAPTER TWENTY

The shuttle took off twenty-eight minutes after it had landed and twenty-two minutes after the four Bugs had died at the farmhouse. Close on two hundred men packed every possible space in the ship, the dead as well as the living. Speed had been the prime essential. The shuttle could not be allowed to stay concealed by the smoke for too long a time without the guardship becoming suspicious, so there had been no time to unload the casualties. The overloaded shuttle had staggered off the ground with an acceleration that was barely two Gs.

But the reduced acceleration should not in itself arouse suspicion, because on the site below the smoke was clearing to show the wide-open lock of the dummy and nothing moving for miles around. They might be worried by the radio breakdown—but the shuttle had, after all, been grounded for less than half an hour, which was short enough time to conduct a rescue operation in dense smoke. And the slow ascent might well be attributed to possibly injured survivors being unable to take high G. Warren moved his gaze from the viewport to the shattered machine-gun blister in the floor and through it to the men packed tightly on the POW decks. He was waiting for the next batch of casualties to appear and wondering if one of them would be himself.

There had been no time to free the wedged-open seals before take-off, and as the vacuum hardened around the climbing ship its atmosphere rushed out of the open locks. Chlorine was just as lethal to the human organism as vacuum, but the drop in pressure would uncover any damage to the helmets or hose connections caused by the violent activity of the assault. From Warren's position in the control-room the POW decks looked as if they were covered with an even layer of up-ended wastepaper baskets, and as he watched some of them began to jerk wildly, and there was a definite fogginess about the place. Warren gritted his teeth as he thought of those men slowly, or not so slowly, strangling to death while their friends within inches of them could do nothing to help. His feelings were so intense that when it became obvious that he himself was not to become a similar casualty his relief was mixed with a definite feeling of guilt . . .

Acceleration ceased. For the next sixty-one minutes they would coast up to the guardship. There would be time to return the damaged antenna to its recess and remove the wedges from the outer seal of the airlock so that outwardly the shuttle would appear in all respects normal. Time also for the pilot to practice on the fine controls prior to making the actual approach, for the lock chamber to be cleared of casualties and for the men to get used to weightlessness.

The Escape site, Andersonstown and the smoke pall all around them shrank to a small grey smudge. In the blackness above the guardship hung like a bright star.

Larger by far than the *Victorious*, at one time a first line battleship of a class which held the record of being the biggest mobile fabrication in space, the guardship was tremendously impressive despite its being forty years obsolete. Lit both by the sun and the dayside of the planet below, it hung like a fat, silvery torpedo whose sleek outline was broken only where the shuttle's dock gaped open to receive them and by the planetary observation platform in the nose. This was a large, glassed-in structure housing the telescopes and detection gear which, in normal operation, remained motionless with respect to the planetary surface while the remainder of the ship rotated for the purpose of supplying the Bugs not on observatory duty with artificial gravity. Since the shuttle was coming in to dock, however, all spin had been killed on the ship.

They crept up to the recessed dock—staggered up was more like it, Warren thought—and magnetic clamps shot out and drew them in. The vast outer seal of the dock folded shut. Several years seemed to pass before pressure built up around their ship and the inner seal opened to allow a crowd of about twelve Bugs to come through. The Bugs had magnets on their feet and four of them were floating stretchers ahead of them, and except for the medics with the stretchers, all wore side-arms. But Warren got the impression that they wore them because it was regulations to do so, and that most of them were present simply because nothing much ever happened on the guardship and this was a break in the routine.

They didn't know how right they were, thought Warren grimly as he banged his wedge with all his force into the bulkhead beside him.

Immediately the escape hatch of the control-room blew open, the reactor inspection panels and all the other emergency exits large enough to allow egress to a man blew also. The main lock and the cargo hatch opened, too, but it was several seconds before anyone could emerge, the reason being the howling gale of chlorine which rushed to fill the vacuum inside the ship. But finally the men came kicking and struggling and almost swimming out of all the exits, and Warren, because he had farther to go than the men leaving by the main lock, arrived when the *mêlée* was well under way.

The Bugs had the initial advantage of being held magnetically to the deck, which allowed them to take a steadier aim and to wreak terrible havoc among the attackers with their explosive bullets. But the advantage was short-lived because the human attackers had mass, inertia and velocity, and they retained these attributes even when they were dead. Warren narrowly avoided being hit by an officer whose head and chest was a cratered ruin and who was spinning slowly and inexorably towards the Bug who had killed him and who, apparently panic-stricken, was pumping more bullets into him in a vain attempt to halt his approach. The ghastly wreckage of the man collided with the Bug and both of them were left spinning helplessly a few feet off the deck. The Bug kept shooting wildly in all directions.

The dock airlock and the corridor beyond it seemed to be solid with struggling, kicking and spinning figures of men and Bugs, with the two stretchers twisting like a pair of fantastic mobiles in the thick of it. It was a mess, an utter shambles. Several times Warren collided violently with men or Bugs and once he felt a sudden, agonizing pain in the calf of his leg, but there was no smell of chlorine in his helmet and the pain grew duller after a few seconds. Explosive pellets flared and cross-bow bolts flickered past everywhere. He kicked past a Bug who had stopped an explosive bullet with its head and three Committee bolts with the rest of its body. He fended off a man with another bolt protruding from the front of his shattered helmet and he fought his way past the grisly remains of both species until he reached the corridor wall. A section of the ship's plumbing ran along the wall and Warren grabbed for it and began pulling himself along it hand over hand until suddenly he was in the clear.

He stopped to catch his breath, to curse the pain in the leg which the bulky shield kept him even from seeing, and to wipe away the sweat from inside his helmet with his forehead pad. The pad was already saturated so that it left foggy streaks on the glass instead of drying it clean, but Warren could see that other men, in steadily increasing numbers were also getting clear.

Singly and in small groups they drifted past him, heading towards Control, Communications, the main reactor or to guard the all-important POW section. He realized suddenly that the obstacle he had just come through had ceased to be a menace, except possibly to navigation. The great mass of bodies still twisted and spun and rebounded off walls and each other—but lifelessly, the shooting had stopped.

He returned briefly to pluck a cross-bow from the air and take a quiver of bolts from an officer who would no longer need them. Feeling sick for a number of reasons, none of which were physiological, Warren set off for the section of the great ship assigned to him to be searched. Five other officers had been given the same duty and he had no way of knowing how many of them were still alive, he knew only that there was very little time to find what he was looking for.

By Warren's reckoning the assault men had about forty minutes air left in their tanks. On average, that was, because the tanks, hose and valves were hand-made and were therefore subject to unavoidable variations in performance —some would have more than an hour left, some considerably less. Inside either of these time limits they might succeed in taking the ship, only to die a few minutes later as their air gave out. Many would be able to make it to the POW section where, because it involved too much time and trouble and waste of oxygen to evacuate and replenish it each time prisoners were transhipped, there was an atmosphere breathable by humans. But that would simply have meant that they were prisoners again. There would have been no way of escaping from that single bubble of oxygen in a chlorine-filled ship, and without the Bugs to work the food synthesizers they would starve.

The next Bug ship to visit the place would be confronted by a terrifying enigma. Their solution to it might very well be to drop a planet-buster on the prison world.

At the thought all the scenes of the past hour returned again in shocking, sickening detail. The bloody shambles inside the shuttle and at the dock, where weightlessness had added a slow-motion, nightmarish quality as well as tripling the casualties, and the relatively quiet and undramatic sight of dozens of men dying because their helmet seals had cracked. Self-doubt as well as self-disgust rose in him again and he had to tell himself sharply that all this had happened exactly as he had planned it—the long preparation and development work, the careful sifting of psychological types, the casualties even. The cost of success, if it came, was high, but the price was well worth it.

Warren moved in a succession of zig-zag dives along the wide, low, brilliantly-lit corridors of the ship, looking into the rooms which opened off them and then hurrying on. This particular section of the guardship was unfamiliar in that only the main corridors had been reproduced as tunnels at Hutton's Mountain, because no amount of psychostimulation of memories or peripheral images had succeeded in gaining data on the purpose or content of these rooms. Some of the corridors had not been reproduced at all.

A Bug appeared suddenly from one of them to crash softly into the wall a few yards ahead of him. Warren jerked up his cross-bow, then relaxed again as he saw the number of bolts already in the target. He kicked himself past the dead Bug and went on with his search.

There was a distinct smell of chlorine in his helmet now. Apparently the blow he'd received on the back of his leg had torn his suit, but the battledress was so tight-fitting at the legs and waist that it had taken some time and a lot of physical activity for the chlorine to begin penetrating to his helmet. As well, his suit wasn't radiating nearly enough of his body heat. He was drowning in his own scalding sweat, his skull seemed ready to crack under the savage pounding of his headache, and the constant jumping and fending-off with his legs and arms was tiring him badly. He had trouble focussing his eyes and he was rapidly slowing down. For minutes at a time he couldn't see where he was going. He diagnosed the trouble as a combination of age, imminent heat-stroke and possible oxygen starvation, and blundered on.

An unguessable time later he opened a door into a large unlighted storeroom, the fan of brightness from the corridor illumination showing that the compartment seemed to be filled with giant bubbles. Warren began pounding out a signal with his wedge on the nearest metal wall, noting as he did so that the symptoms which had been troubling him were still present, but sharply diminished in severity.

Twenty minutes later he had a relay set up between the storeroom and the POW quarters and was pushing helmets, air-tanks and med-kits along it as fast as he could. As many as eight helmets were drifting down the corridor at one time, to be picked out of the air by the man stationed at the other end of it and given another push along the next leg of their journey. There were several hundred fish-bowls and regulation attachments for service battledress in the storeroom, and Warren knew that if he had time to check serial numbers he would find his own in the pile, because every prisoner who was processed by the guardship had to leave his helmet behind. The Bugs must have had thousands of helmets left with them since the POW planet had been initiated, and it had been natural to assume that they would stack them somewhere until sheer numbers made them a nuisance and they were destroyed. The Committee had taken a gamble on this, but it had come off. By the look of this storeroom the Bugs didn't spring-clean too often.

Kelso and two other officers arrived, and while the others relieved Warren in the storeroom the Lieutenant proffered a Bug pad on which he had written with a Bug stylus the news that the main centres of the guardship had been secured. As a postscript he had added that the Marshal's air must be running low and respectfully suggested that he conduct him to the prisoners' quarters. Warren scribbled out his approval both of the Lieutenant's report and suggestion, and together they launched themselves along the corridor.

It happened at the third intersection. Warren had just checked his last jump with his feet against the wall when there was suddenly no air to breathe. He sucked desperately but his lungs weren't getting anything. His chest was on fire, a throbbing, black cloud cut off his sight of the corridor, even of the sweat-smeared interior of his helmet, and his head began to pound louder and louder until the sound became a series of monstrous, thudding explosions.

After all I've come through, he raged silently, *what a way to die . . .!*

He felt Kelso grip his arm and he twisted frantically, the instincts of a drowning man making him kick and claw and hold on for grim life. He felt his fingers sink into the wickerwork of Kelso's suit, felt the thin canes bend and break under his frenzied grip. A tiny, sane portion of his mind told him that he was endangering the Lieutenant's seals with his struggles, had perhaps already condemned Kelso to death with him, but the tiny area of sanity was overwhelmed and obliterated by sheer panic . . .

He came to with the slightly sour air of the prisoners' section rushing into his lungs, its progress only slightly impeded by the fingers being held loosely over his mouth. Kelso was astride his chest, his helmet was smashed open in front and the Lieutenant's fingers were there to prevent Warren breathing in the broken glass which was floating about. He tapped Kelso's arm to let him know that he was all right, and grinning the Lieutenant let go and carefully smashed in the front of his own helmet with a wedge. Together they began chipping at the seals.

It was sheer bliss to wriggle out of the ungainly contraption of basketwork and glass and to be able to twist and to bend at the waist again. All over the vast room the men were struggling out of the baskets and revelling briefly, very briefly, in their freedom before clamping on service helmets and six-hour tanks to rush away again to relieve men still holding vital positions in wicker suits, or to search the area for people who had run out of air on the way in. There were a lot of cases like that, Warren saw; men who had to be broken out of their armour and given artificial respiration, or have their hearts shocked back into motion with a shot from the med kits. And there were those who did not respond. They drifted weightless and outwardly unharmed about the room, having missed victory and life by only a few minutes. Warren felt particularly bad about them.

He became aware that Kelso was staring at his leg. Warren twisted around to see what the other was looking at and discovered a cross-bow bolt neatly transfixing his left calf. He began to laugh and found that he had to make a tremendous effort to stop. He drew the injured leg up to where he could work on it, then carefully removed the flights from the bolt and pulled it free. He wanted to yell out loud with the pain of it, but he kept his face impassive and the only sound he made was caused by heavy breathing through his nose.

After his shameful display of panic in the corridor and his fit of hysterical laughter in here, Warren felt that he had to do something to retrieve his reputation in Kelso's eyes. His behaviour in the corridor had been bad, even cowardly. It wasn't as if he was the only man to run out of air today. And now he had to pretend that he wasn't the gutless individual that he knew himself to be.

He held the bolt where the Lieutenant could see it, then he said drily, 'And all the time I thought the men liked me . . .'

'Oh they *do*, sir!' said Kelso.

Warren looked away from the Lieutenant's face quickly, feeling embarrassed. It was wrong that a mature, intelligent, resourceful and very brave man like Kelso should look at him the way a dog looks at its master.

An hour later, Warren, in service lightweight suit with long-duration tanks, sound diaphragms and a measure of air-conditioning, was searching the ship again. His party included Kelso and the officer who had piloted the shuttle. On the surface it looked as if they had won, but the guardship was a very large vessel and somewhere inside it there might be a Bug desperate with the knowledge of defeat who was planning something calamitous in the way of destruction for itself and its ship, not to mention the prisoners it contained. This time the whole ship was being searched. Thoroughly.

It was Warren's party who found the last Bug survivors. There were two of them in the compartment, spacesuited but unarmed. Around them floated three pressure litters, the type of stretcher with plastic envelope used for transporting casualties in airless conditions, and in each one of them there was an oily, pallid, twitching, *something*. It took a few seconds for them to realize what it was they were seeing.

'If there's anything in the Galaxy more horrible-looking than a Bug,' said Kelso finally, 'it's a young Bug . . .'

CHAPTER TWENTY-ONE

The first thing Warren did after transferring the Bug prisoners to their quarters in Hutton's Mountain was to move Peters and Hubbard to the guardship. He had a long talk with the political officer, during which Hubbard came to see things his way, then released him safe in the knowledge that the other would not talk out of turn. With Peters it was different. Warren saw to it that the Fleet Commander had every possible comfort except that of conversation, but he had no intention of talking to Peters until he was good and ready. He could not risk having Peters throw a spanner in the works at this late stage. And with the Commander rendered harmless he was able to devote all of his attention to the ship and to the officers who would man her.

He made it quite clear from the first that the ship would be *manned*.

Warren himself did not leave the ship, although he kept in touch with Fielding and Hynds by the Bug radio equipment taken from the battleship. He needed Hynds to track down information of obsolete Earth and Bug weapons and control-systems and Fielding, perhaps unknown to herself, was supplying the psychological know-how which was helping him to separate the sheep from the wolves. Hutton visited the ship many times.

The Major expressed deep concern over the age, appointments and general condition of the vessel, at the same time giving forth with a constant stream of suggestions as to how the hopelessly obsolete equipment might be thrown away, modified or completely rebuilt to the best advantage. It was his considered opinion that the great, fat sow of a ship would disintegrate the moment thrust was applied and that its weapons were a deadlier menace to the ordnance officers than to any target, but at the same time the hints he let drop to Warren about wanting to go along were many and quite unsubtle. Knowing that Hutton was merely reacting to the magnitude of the technical challenge of making the ship operational again, and that the Major had become too much of a pacifist to really fit into the ship's crew, Warren's treatment of these hints was equally unsubtle. He said 'No'.

And so the days passed into weeks, with the shuttle plying between the ship and the surface as often as twice a day. Going down it carried Bug provisions for their prisoners, all the Bug literature, records, charts, electronics and optical equipment together with all the machine tools and mechanical oddments which could be spared. Coming back it brought food, the chosen Committeemen and hundreds of trays of the weed which Hutton had developed to supply the ship with air. Gradually the chlorine was bled into space, and deck by deck it was replaced by oxygen-rich air until the entire circulation system carried a human rather than a Bug atmosphere. The work of modifying and provisioning the ship accelerated rapidly after that.

Interior lighting was toned down to a comfortable intensity. Where necessary the Bug controls were reshaped to suit human hands and, so far as was possible considering their present close proximity to the planet, their weapons were tested. The men were fast getting used to ceilings which gave only a few inches of head-room, to sitting cross-legged in Bug chairs and to sleeping in the big oval beds which were like over-padded hammocks. Warren had given permission for anyone who needed them to have necessary items of furniture brought up in the shuttle, but he discovered that there was a widespread feeling among the men that anyone who couldn't sit in a Bug chair or sleep in a Bug bed was something of a sissy.

Morale among the entire crew was very high and it was

152

clear that no good purpose would be served by remaining in orbit around the ex-prison planet any longer, so on E-Day plus eighty-four Warren went down in the shuttle to give his final instructions and to say good-bye.

He took Peters and Kelso with him, and when they landed he told the Lieutenant that he would be back in an hour and to wait for him at the ship. He had a lot to tell the Fleet Commander and none of what he had to say was for the ears of Kelso or any of the other hide-bound Committeemen on the guardship, so Warren talked a lot during the walk from the shuttle to the ruins of Andersonstown. But the Commander did very little talking back. Perhaps the reason lay in the devastation around them and the acrid, burnt smell which still hung in the air, or maybe it was simply that the Commander was too shocked at what the Marshal was confessing to for him to discuss it just yet.

They entered the building chosen for this final meeting, a storehouse near the harbour which was one of the first to be rebuilt. Inside the benches were filled with the more active anti-Committee officers, the higher level technicians from the mountain and the other members of Warren's staff. He knew that his face looked grim as he took up his position with the Fleet Commander behind the table before them, and set the fish-bowl he had been carrying down on the table. The prospect of a confession is never a pleasant one, and Warren alone knew how much he had to confess.

Harshly, he began, 'We will leave as soon as I return to the ship. Before saying good-bye I have certain, hu, explanations and instructions for you. The first is that any officers among you who are planning how best to avoid the rescue force and a return to active service can relax. I will not be back for you. Nobody will be back for you, ever . . .'

The expressions of wary hostility had changed suddenly to bewilderment, and Warren wondered if the gulf which had opened between these people and himself over the past months could be closed by a few minutes conversation. It would be nice if it could, but standing in his trim battle-dress uniform among all the kilts and shapeless leather pants he felt so alien and different that he might have been a Bug facing them.

'The reason for this is a situation which was apparent

153

even before I was taken prisoner,' Warren continued, 'although it surprised me that the total collapse of our military organization could come about in the three years that I've been here. However it did happen. The service broke up through political mismanagement and wholesale desertions and the simple shortage of proper officers and maintenance technicians. The Fleet Commander will confirm that we have up-to-date and accurate intelligence in this matter. Even in my time this process was so well advanced that the possibility of the prisoners here being rescued was an extremely remote one, despite all that I said, or led you to believe, to the contrary.

'Knowing this, my decision to back the Escape Committee requires some explanation . . .'

Very briefly Warren outlined again the situation on the prison planet as he had seen it on arrival; the two mutually hostile groups whose dislike was on the point of flaring into violence, the breakdown of discipline and respect for authority and the apparent ascendency of the Civilian over the Committee side which was simply driving the Committeemen into a tighter and more fanatical group. The considerable authority and ability of the Fleet Commander, aided by environmental factors and the purely biological forces at work—and here it should be said that the prisoners were held to the planet much more tightly by their growing number of children than by the Bug guardship—was unable to control these fanatics who placed loyalty to the service and their responsibilities as officers before comfort and security and female companionship. They placed Honour above all else, and Warren had decided that the only way to control such narrow-minded yet admirable men was to join them and lead them in the general direction in which they wanted to go.

Not to have done so would have resulted in an Escape Committee, so shrunken in size that it would be plain even to themselves that escape was impossible, which had tight communications and organization, turning on the Civilians who had betrayed them. The Civilians were in the majority but were not organized at all. After many years, perhaps many generations of strife the situation would have found its own level, but in the process all the valuable skills and

154

knowledge of the prisoners would have been lost. In a very short time the planet would have been populated by little more than savages.

By siding with the Committee he had caused the second continent to be opened up, which in turn forced into being the network of communications and commerce by ship, glider and helio relay. None of this would have been possible without Committee drive and organization. He had also, by lying outrageously regarding his reasons for wanting it, caused a vast amount of technology to be recorded and distributed in written form, and he had set up the machinery for self training and teaching. The result was that there was now little likelihood of their knowledge, particularly the space and related technologies, dying with them. In any event the Bug gadgetry he was leaving behind would ensure its being kept alive.

There had been times when Warren had wanted to do it the Fleet Commander's way, especially during those long periods when the Civilians and Committeemen seemed to be getting along well together. But then one of his men would say something, or there would be a beating-up or some thoughtless destruction of Civilian property, and Warren would realize that there was no easy way out. Undermining the Committee from within was simply carrying on the job which the Fleet Commander had started, and the result would have been equally unsatisfactory. His men were potential troublemakers whether they called themselves Civilians or Committeemen. They were the type of men who made history, usually of the wrong sort. They were the wolves among the sheep. The only thing to do with wolves was to get rid of them, one way or another . . .

'. . . There was always a strong possibility that the Bugs would realize at the last moment that the site was an ambush,' Warren continued, 'and dump a missile on us. That was my reserve plan if the first one failed. It would have been a dramatically simple way of disposing of the wolves, because it was the most loyal Committeemen who stayed on the site during the final hours. But these were fine men—good, able officers who were not to blame for what they were and the trouble they might ultimately cause. The fact that they sometimes went off the rails a bit with

155

Civilians and some of the female officers didn't make me feel any better about sentencing them to death, because I knew, and so did they, what a bloody massacre even a successful escape would be. I liked those men and wanted to kill as few of them as possible.

'What I mean is they weren't very gentle or thoughtful people,' Warren went on awkwardly, 'but they had enthusiasm and they would never admit that anything was impossible. They still won't and I still like them. What they tried to do . . . what we *did* do was . . . was . . .'

'Glorious,' said Peters softly.

Warren looked quickly at the Fleet Commander, suspecting sarcasm, but he was mistaken. For several seconds he stared down at his helmet, unable to speak.

'What will you do now, sir?' said Hutton quietly.

Clearing his throat, Warren said, 'Our interstellar culture, along with that of the Bugs, is in the process of falling apart. I have a large ship in reasonably good condition. I have upwards of one thousand men aboard who, both crew and assault commandos, are personally loyal to me, and I have an officer capable of advising me on the political aspects of any situation. It should be possible for us to cut ourselves a chunk of this disintegrating culture, hold it and impose on it some sort of order which would halt or possibly reverse the tendency to regress towards savagery which occurs with isolated colonies previously dependent on the mother world. That is what I will try to do. Meanwhile, you will have a much harder job.

'If you don't believe that,' he went on grimly, 'just think for a minute what exactly it is that you are.'

Warren stared hard into the faces before him, because the bloody, nightmarish pictures which were always on the fringe of his mental vision were trying to take form again in the air between them, and this was the only way he had of fighting it. He was telling them the reason why one hundred and forty-two assault men had died—the *real* reason, not just the one that the men themselves had thought they had.

He said, 'You are a planet of scientifically trained, psychologically stable and highly intelligent human beings who have, so far as was possible, had all the unstable and

156

unsane influences removed from among you. You are in a unique position, therefore, and I expect a lot from you and your descendants. Some of you may have thought that you were ducking your responsibilities by going civilian, but this isn't so. You have obligations immeasurably stronger and deeper than any simple oath of service, the respons-ibility of the civilized person towards the savage, of the haves for the have-nots.

'I cannot tell you in detail what you should do,' Warren continued. 'My advice is that you remain underground, so far as technology is concerned, for another ten years so as to be on the safe side if a Bug ship should turn up—but my guess is that if one doesn't arrive within the next three years it won't come at all. Meanwhile you will be keeping alive the science of an interstellar culture and seeing to it that the kids who are beginning to clutter up the place learn a lot more than wood-carving—a whole lot more! At the same time you will try to love and cherish and treat as your very own those Bug prisoners at the mountain. You will see to it that they are healthy and comfortable and as happy as possible so that they will not be averse to breeding in captivity like ourselves. You will then see to it that your own darling children get plenty of chances to see theirs— you could arrange it like a visit to the zoo, at first, but later you will teach them to respect these chlorine-breathers and to communicate with them. There will be difficulties, of course, but it isn't entirely impossible for a youngster to make friends with his bogey-man. You have some very good psychologists here . . .'

The picture forming before him now was from a bright and, he hoped, not too distant future rather than from the immediate and bloody past. Firmly, he went on, 'Even-tually—in six or seven generations from now, perhaps— you will be ready to go out. All around you will be the fragments of two promising interstellar cultures who met before either was ready for a meeting. Your job will be to pick up the pieces, *all* the pieces, and put them together again.

'With any luck,' he added hopefully, 'one of the biggest and most civilized pieces might have been mine . . .'

They were all staring at him, Fielding, Hutton, Hynds

and the others, as if he was something new and frightening, something accepted as a known quantity which had turned suddenly and bitten them. Warren saw now that his confession of lying and treachery and wholesale double dealing was of secondary importance, that he had given them something much more important to think about. The fact that they did consider it more important, and the expressions on their faces as they stared through him and into space and future time, told Warren what he wanted to know. The job would be done. He was content.

'Well,' he said finally, lifting his helmet and turning to go, 'I guess that's it, then . . .'

Kelso burst into the room a few seconds later, in a near panic because the Marshal had been gone longer than the stipulated hour and the Lieutenant had begun to think that harm had come to him at the hands of the Civilians. The Lieutenant was in time to see a sight so mind-staggering that he felt himself guilty of a most unmilitary gape. It was the sight of a roomful of Civilians standing rigidly to attention while the Fleet Commander, old man Peters himself, tore off a salute to the Marshal which was the tightest, smartest and plainly the most respectful salute that Kelso had ever seen.

A SELECTION OF FINE READING AVAILABLE IN CORGI BOOKS

Novels

- ☐ 552 08395 X DEAR DR DALE — *Jonquil Antony* 4/-
- ☐ 552 08351 8 TELL ME HOW LONG THE TRAIN'S BEEN GONE — *James Baldwin* 7/-
- ☐ 552 08506 5 A RAGING CALM — *Stan Barstow* 7/-
- ☐ 552 07938 3 THE NAKED LUNCH — *William Burroughs* 7/6
- ☐ 552 08465 4 THE SOFT MACHINE — *William Burroughs* 7/-
- ☐ 552 08492 1 TOBACCO ROAD — *Erskine Caldwell* 5/-
- ☐ 552 08562 6 GOD'S LITTLE ACRE — *Erskine Caldwell* 5/-
- ☐ 552 08493 X THE LONG CORRIDOR — *Catherine Cookson* 5/-
- ☐ 552 08561 8 THE UNBAITED TRAP — *Catherine Cookson* 5/-
- ☐ 552 08183 3 BOYS AND GIRLS TOGETHER — *William Goldman* 7/6
- ☐ 552 07968 5 THE WELL OF LONELINESS — *Radclyffe Hall* 7/6
- ☐ 552 08125 6 CATCH-22 — *Joseph Heller* 7/-
- ☐ 552 08507 3 THE HERITAGE — *Frances Parkinson Keyes* 6/-
- ☐ 552 08524 3 THE KITES OF WAR — *Derek Lambert* 5/-
- ☐ 552 08560 X BLOSSOM LIKE THE ROSE — *Norah Lofts* 6/-
- ☐ 552 08466 2 HERE WAS A MAN — *Norah Lofts* 6/-
- ☐ 552 08442 5 THE AU PAIR BOY — *Andrew McCall* 6/-
- ☐ 552 08002 0 MY SISTER, MY BRIDE — *Edwina Mark* 5/-
- ☐ 552 08467 0 ALMOST AN AFFAIR — *Nan Maynard* 6/-
- ☐ 552 08502 2 CARAVANS — *James A. Michener* 7/-
- ☐ 552 08564 2 VENUS IN PLASTIC — *James Mitchell* 4/-
- ☐ 552 08124 9 LOLITA — *Vladmir Nabokov* 6/-
- ☐ 552 08525 1 THE MARIGOLD FIELD — *Diane Pearson* 6-
- ☐ 552 08491 3 PRETTY MAIDS ALL IN A ROW — *Francis Pollini* 7/-
- ☐ 552 07954 5 RUN FOR THE TREES — *James Rand* 7/
- ☐ 552 08392 5 SOMETHING OF VALUE — *Robert Ruark* 8/-
- ☐ 552 08509 X THE CROWDED BED — *Henry Sackerman* 6/-
- ☐ 552 08372 0 LAST EXIT TO BROOKLYN — *Hubert Selby Jr.* 10/-
- ☐ 552 08526 X FEEL FREE — *David Slavitt* 5/-
- ☐ 552 07807 7 VALLEY OF THE DOLLS — *Jacqueline Susann* 8/-
- ☐ 552 08523 5 THE LOVE MACHINE — *Jacqueline Susann* 8/-
- ☐ 552 08013 6 THE EXHIBITIONIST — *Henry Sutton* 7/6
- ☐ 552 08217 1 THE CARETAKERS — *Dariel Telfer* 7/-
- ☐ 552 08091 8 TOPAZ — *Leon Uris* 8/-
- ☐ 552 08383 4 EXODUS — *Leon Uris* 8/-
- ☐ 552 08563 4 THE KING'S MISTRESS — *Julia Watson* 4/-
- ☐ 552 08073 X THE PRACTICE — *Stanley Winchester* 8/-
- ☐ 552 08391 7 MEN WITH KNIVES — *Stanley Winchester* 7/-
- ☐ 552 07116 1 FOREVER AMBER Vol. I — *Kathleen Winsor* 5/-
- ☐ 552 07117 X FOREVER AMBER Vol. II — *Kathleen Winsor* 5/-
- ☐ 552 08539 1 THE BEFORE MIDNIGHT SCHOLAR — *Li Yu* 8/-

War

- ☐ 552 08487 5 SIGNED WITH THEIR HONOUR — *James Aldridge* 7/-
- ☐ 552 08565 0 BATTLE OF THE APRIL STORM — *Larry Forrester* 5/-
- ☐ 552 08551 0 ONE MAN'S WARS — *Gilbert Hackforth-Jones* 5/-
- ☐ 552 08552 9 CHINESE POISON — *Gilbert Hackforth-Jones* 5/-
- ☐ 552 08528 6 MARCH BATTALION — *Sven Hassel* 6/-
- ☐ 552 08496 4 JIM BRADY—LEADING SEAMAN — *J. E. Macdonnell* 5/-
- ☐ 552 98558 9 FOURTEEN EIGHTEEN — *John Masters* 21/-
- ☐ 552 08536 7 THE SCOURGE OF THE SWASTIKA — *Lord Russell* 6/-
- ☐ 552 08537 5 THE KNIGHTS OF BUSHIDO — *Lord Russell* 6/-
- ☐ 552 08470 0 UNOFFICIAL HISTORY — *Field-Marshal Sir William Slim* 5/-
- ☐ 552 08527 8 THE LONG DROP — *Alan White* 5/-

Romance

- ☐ 552 08515 4 THE HEALING TIME — *Lucilla Andrews* 4/-
- ☐ 552 08569 3 ST. JULIAN'S DAY — *Bess Norton* 4/-
- ☐ 552 08477 8 A STRANGER IN TOWN — *Alex Stuart* 4/-

Science Fiction

☐ 552 08516 2	NEW WRITINGS IN SF 17	John Carnell	5/-
☐ 552 08499 9	REACH FOR TOMORROW	Arthur C. Clarke	5/-
☐ 552 08453 0	DRAGONFLIGHT	Anne McCaffrey	5/-
☐ 552 08401 8	A CANTICLE FOR LEIBOWITZ	Walter M. Miller Jr.	6/-
☐ 552 08478 6	LOGAN'S RUN William F. Nolan and George Clayton-Johnson		4/-
☐ 552 08500 6	THE INNER LANDSCAPE	Peake/Ballard/Aldiss	5/-
☐ 552 08533 2	EARTH ABIDES	George R. Stewart	6/-

General

☐ 552 98434 5	GOODBYE BABY AND AMEN David Bailey and Peter Evans		25/-
☐ 552 07566 3	SEXUAL LIFE IN ENGLAND	Dr. Ivan Bloch	9/6
☐ 552 08403 4	LIFE IN THE WORLD UNSEEN	Anthony Borgia	5/-
☐ 552 07593 0	UNMARRIED LOVE	Dr. Eustace Chesser	5/-
☐ 552 07950 2	SEXUAL BEHAVIOUR	Dr. Eustace Chesser	5/-
☐ 552 08402 6	SEX AND THE MARRIED WOMAN	Dr. Eustace Chesser	7/-
☐ 552 98572 4	NEE DE LA VAGUE (illustrated)	Lucien Clergue	21/-
☐ 552 07400 4	MY LIFE AND LOVES	Frank Harris	13/-
☐ 552 98121 4	FIVE GIRLS (illus. rated)	Sam Haskins	21/-
☐ 552 97745 4	COWBOY KATE (illustrated)	Sam Haskins	21/-
☐ 552 08362 3	A DOCTOR SPEAKS ON SEXUAL EXPRESSION IN MARRIAGE	Donald W. Hastings, M.D.	10/-
☐ 552 98247 4	THE HISTORY OF THE NUDE IN PHOTOGRAPHY (illustrated) Peter Lacey and Anthony La Rotonda		25/-
☐ 552 98345 4	THE ARTIST AND THE NUDE (illustrated)		21/-
☐ 552 08069 1	THE OTHER VICTORIANS	Steven Marcus	10/-
☐ 552 08010 1	THE NAKED APE	Desmond Morris	6/-
☐ 552 07965 0	SOHO NIGHT AND DAY (illustrated)	Norman and Bernard	7/6
☐ 552 08105 1	BEYOND THE TENTH	T. Lobsang Rampa	5/-
☐ 552 08228 7	WOMAN: a Biological Study	Philip Rhodes	5/-
☐ 552 98178 8	THE YELLOW STAR (illustrated)	Gerhard Schoenberner	21/-
☐ 552 08456 5	COMPLETE BOOK OF JUKADO SELF-DEFENCE (illustrated)	Bruce Tegner	6/-
☐ 552 98479 5	MADEMOISELLE 1 + 1 (illustrated) Marcel Veronese and Jean-Claude Peretz		21/-

Western

☐ 552 08532 4	BLOOD BROTHER	Elliott Arnold	8/-
☐ 552 08567 7	SUDDEN—DEAD OR ALIVE	Frederick H. Christian	4/-
☐ 552 08531 6	BACK TO THE BLOODY BORDER	J. T. Edson	4/-
☐ 552 08451 4	THE OWLHOOT	J. T. Edson	4/-
☐ 552 08514 6	ALIAS BUTCH CASSIDY	Will Henry	4/-
☐ 552 08475 1	NO SURVIVORS	Will Henry	5/-
☐ 552 08485 9	THE FIRST FAST DRAW	Louis L'Amour	4/-
☐ 552 08476 X	GALLOWAY	Louis L'Amour	4/-
☐ 552 08574 X	FLINT	Louis L'Amour	4/-
☐ 552 08575 8	MOJAVE CROSSING	Louis L'Amour	4/-
☐ 552 08568 5	MAVERICKS	Jack Schaefer	4/-

Crime

☐ 552 08530 8	THE PROBLEM OF THE WIRE CAGE	John Dickson Carr	4/-
☐ 552 08554 5	FIND THE BODY	John Creasey	5/-
☐ 552 08555 3	FIRST A MURDER	John Creasey	5/-
☐ 552 08316 X	FOUNDER MEMBER	John Gardner	5/-
☐ 552 08513 8	A COOL DAY FOR KILLING	William Haggard	4/-
☐ 552 08472 7	THE INNOCENT BYSTANDERS	James Munro	5/-
☐ 552 08520 0	KISS ME, DEADLY	Mickey Spillane	4/-
☐ 552 08425 5	THE SHADOW GAME	Michael Underwood	4/-

All these books are available at your book shop or newsagent; or can be ordered direct from the publisher. Just tick the titles you want and fill in the form below.

CORGI BOOKS, Cash Sales Department, P.O. Box 11, Falmouth, Cornwall.
Please send cheque or postal order. No currency, and allow 6d. per book to cover the cost of postage and packing in U.K., 9d. per copy overseas.

NAME..

ADDRESS..

(NOV, '70)...